THE CASE OF THE

BESIEGED
BASSO

THE CASE OF THE

BESIEGED BASSO

an Augusta McKee mystery

Susan Moore Jordan

ISBN: 978-1-950625-35-2

Published by Shaggy Dog Productions, LLC

Cover design and art by Wesley Goulart

Books by Susan Moore Jordan

The *Carousel* Trilogy:
How I Grew Up
Eli's Heart
You Are My Song

Jamie's Children

The Cameron Saga:
Memories of Jake
Man with No Yesterdays
And This Shall Be for Music

"More Fog, Please"
(non-fiction)

Augusta McKee Mysteries:
The Case of the Slain Soprano
The Case of the Disappearing Director
The Case of the Toxic Tenor
The Case of the Purloined Professor
The Case of the Chrysanthemum Murders
The Case of the Unearthed Evidence
The Case of the 'Carousel' Killer
The Case of the Bogus Beatle
The Case of the Casanova Cantor
The Case of the Ill-Fated Philanthropist
The Case of the Besieged Basso

Table of Contents

To all our military veterans,
Especially those from the
Vietnam conflict.
May they find peace and comfort.

Prologue
A Man with a Mission

Thursday, March 5, 1970

8:30 p.m. He glanced at the gun lying next to him. It wouldn't be much longer. He slid down further in the car seat, pulling his cap over his eyes, trying to relax as much as possible.

He had parked across the street from his target's apartment house, in front of a closed store. Ironically, a sporting goods store, a store where he could have bought the gun. But that pistol had traveled far with him. He knew it was dependable, and he wasn't going to switch now.

He'd been sure to park between streetlights, where the darkness offered more concealment. Across the street, the light above the main entrance of the apartment building wasn't working. The man he followed had parked on the same side as the apartment building, further up the street.

The gunman was dressed in black—black pants, black shirt, black jacket. Black cap. Black gloves. It was a dark night, no moon, no stars. A hint of rain or snow in the air.

The night felt so peaceful he nearly dozed off but shook himself awake. Again he touched the gun; just yesterday he had taken it into the woods to ensure it was working perfectly.

Footsteps headed his way.

He slid down even further, listening, holding his breath, trying to make himself invisible. The footsteps grew louder but didn't hesitate, moving past him and fading away in the distance.

9:05 p.m. Movement at the apartment building door. Wide awake, the gunman watched as the man exited and moved toward his car.

He waited until he heard the car pull away before leaving his vehicle and heading for the entrance, first making sure no one was around.

Swiftly up the carpeted stairs to the second floor. He crept down the hall to Apartment 2C, silently inserting the key he had made into the lock, turning it slowly and steadily.

His target stood in the kitchen, washing dishes at the sink, his back to the door. The gunman carefully eased the front door closed, not making a sound, and entered the kitchen.

"You thought you got away with it, didn't you?" he hissed.

He watched the man abruptly turn around, surprise and then fear on his face. The gun, muffled by a silencer, discharged twice. The gunman heard the *thunk! thunk!* as his victim collapsed to the floor. Two fatal shots to the heart. He knelt beside the victim, pressing fingers to the carotid artery. No pulse.

The gunman returned to the front door, turned the knob and listened. Not a sound in the hallway. Leaving the door to the apartment unlocked and slightly ajar, he moved quickly down the stairs, out the exit, across the street.

Inside his car, a slow, satisfied smile spread across his face. He drove away, confident no one would ever know he had been there.

Chapter One
The Ultimate Operatic Villain

A week earlier
Saturday, February 28, 1970

Glorious voices filled the rehearsal room in Cincinnati's Music Hall on a cold Saturday afternoon in February. This was a first vocal run-through of the "Antonia" act of Offenbach's *The Tales of Hoffmann*, but Augusta McKee could already visualize how amazing this performance would be in a few short weeks with a full orchestra, the singers in costume, the room filled with appreciative audience. She sighed happily and hugged herself.

Conductor Thomas Schippers, acting as accompanist for this rehearsal, saw her reaction and smiled warmly. He knew Augusta still had a difficult time believing the Board of Directors had invited her to direct this production. It certainly was a large step up from directing student productions at the Conservatory and Cliffside College, and she felt hugely complimented.

The title role of Hoffmann, a young German university student, would be performed by tenor Jamie Logan, a graduate of the Conservatory who had become a premier tenor in Opera World. Due to his busy schedule, he wouldn't be joining them until the week before the performances. Augusta filled in for him at this rehearsal, occasionally singing some of his lines.

Aside from the title role, Augusta had been free to cast the other characters in the opera. Her first choice for the demanding role of the villain was Allan Meissner, former Conservatory student, presently a voice teacher at the school, and soon to audition as a finalist in the Metropolitan Opera National Auditions. Allan had performed this act in an opera workshop production while a student some six years earlier. Soprano Martha Mitchell, singing the role of Antonia, had also been part of that cast.

Maestro Schippers paused the rehearsal briefly to give a few notes to the singers. Augusta looked over her own notes for staging. She was excited for Allan and thrilled by how well he was vocally portraying this villainous character. Any basso who performed the villain in *The Tales of Hoffmann* was challenged to create four distinct personalities, one for each act: a sophisticate; a pseudo-scientist; a master manipulator, and finally, the murderous Dr. Miracle.

Allan and Augusta had discussed this complex and demanding role more than once, and she reminded him how well he had performed Dr. Miracle in that opera workshop production years earlier.

"You were outstanding even then. An amazing performance for an undergrad student."

"You think so? My memory is that I was nervous the entire time I was onstage. No doubt you recall what a rookie I was as an actor." He laughed. "But I did love singing this and hoped someday I might perform the entire opera."

Augusta nodded. "We talked then about the difficulties in this role. It was challenging for you when we only performed the 'Antonia' act to arrive at the ultimate villainy of Miracle. It's much more satisfying to perform the first three iterations of the character and build to this one. I'm so happy for you that you have this opportunity to do exactly that, and I'm hearing subtle differences in your voice in each of the acts."

Allan had flipped through his score. "You know, I've read a theory that each of these characters actually represents the darker side of Hoffmann himself. The thought that he's his own worst enemy manifested in these four onstage characters."

Augusta brought her attention back to turning pages for Thomas Schippers, thinking again how privileged Cincinnati was to have him in their city on a more permanent basis these days as Musical Director of the Cincinnati Symphony Orchestra. A fast-rising star in the world of music, Schippers had conducted opera all over Europe and at the major opera houses in the United States. Energetic and charismatic, he captivated everyone he worked with. And it didn't hurt that the man was movie-star handsome: tall, trim, with charm to spare.

Schippers brought the act to a close, standing to applaud his singers.

"Remarkable. You are all absolutely spot on in these roles. What a pleasure to work with you," he beamed. As the singers began to disperse, he thanked Augusta for filling in for Jamie Logan as Hoffmann.

"I'll tell Jamie to watch out. I may be taking over his role," Augusta laughed.

Schippers marked a few items in his score and then placed it in his briefcase. "It's truly a pleasure to work with you, Augusta. And my heartfelt compliments on the quality of these young singers. You're a great teacher."

"I try to help them understand what they need to do," Augusta replied. "It's my privilege to be able to do that, especially when there is so much natural talent."

"Walk you to your car, Augusta?" Allan stood beside her. At nearly six feet six inches, he was one of the few men she was forced to look up to, since in her signature stiletto heels she was six feet one.

She glanced up at him, thinking how the slightly gawky teenager she first knew had grown into an attractive man. "You're singing incredibly these days. I have high hopes for the Met audition."

He grinned. "From your lips to the gods of music's ears. I'm not counting on anything, but I like the fact a lot of people in the business will hear me sing. I'm eager to perform."

They had reached her car parked just in front of Music Hall, and Allan glanced for several moments in both directions.

"Were you expecting someone?" she asked.

"Not…really." Allan looked off into the distance. "I've had this strange feeling lately that I can't seem to shake. As if someone is watching me. Or following me." A rueful grin. "That's nonsense, isn't it?"

"Do you feel it often?" Augusta felt a sympathetic flutter in her chest.

"More often than I'd like. It does make me uneasy."

She rested a hand on his arm. "Allan, you're a Vietnam combat veteran. You are more attuned to a sense of danger than the average person."

"Or maybe more paranoid than the average person?"

"No, really, Allan, if you've felt this often, why not report it to the police? It couldn't hurt."

"I might do that. But why would someone be following me? That just doesn't make any sense. And what could the police do? I'll stay alert when I have this feeling, and if I have something more concrete I'll talk to the police."

This remained in Augusta's mind as she went into her house in Hyde Park. She was greeted effusively at the door by her Golden Shepherd, Fritz. The wonderful aroma of coffee greeted her as well, and her husband, Malcolm Mitchell, recently promoted to Acting Commander of the newly formed Criminal Investigations Section of the Cincinnati Police Department, called out from the alcove.

"In here, Gus."

Augusta relaxed into a chair as Malcolm placed coffee and a croissant on the table. "I thought you might need some sustenance after your session with Thomas Schippers."

"Malcolm, he is absolutely the best. What an incredible experience to be working with him at this early stage of just reviewing music. I can't wait to have the full cast together and begin staging the opera. Cincinnati is so, so fortunate that he agreed to come here."

Two sugars and a healthy splash of cream for Augusta. Black for Malcom, the ultimate tough guy cop. Yet it had been his beautiful dark blue eyes that first attracted her. That and his rugged good looks: firm jaw and muscular but trim physique.

"Yes, especially since the Summer Opera plans to move from the Zoo to Music Hall within the next two years," he said.

"I have mixed feelings about that. I love opera at the Zoo. There's nothing like it."

Mal laughed. "If you mean hearing elephants, tigers, lions, and other assorted animal sounds during the performance of an opera, you certainly are right about that. On the flip side, larger audiences in Music Hall. A bigger stage. A larger orchestra if necessary. You can't dismiss air-conditioning and no rain."

"Oh, I know all the arguments for moving." Augusta swallowed her bite of croissant. "Better parking. Much better backstage accommodations for the singers. I'm still stunned that I was invited to direct *Hoffmann*, and I hope it means there may be more such invitations. I'll definitely miss after parties at Mecklenburg's, though."

"That doesn't have to happen. It's easy to drive from Music Hall to Mt. Auburn for a great restaurant. It's not that far."

Augusta glanced through the window at her garden, resting for the winter in the late afternoon's gathering darkness. The alcove was her favorite room in the house. One wall of windows, another with a glass door which opened into the living room. The room had an airy, peaceful feeling. She had bought the comfortable, attractive Tudor a few years before she met Malcolm. He eventually moved in with her and they had celebrated their wedding in this house five years ago. Together, they had made it home.

"I take it Martha did well?" Malcolm asked, referring to his daughter-in-law, Martha, now married to his detective son Danny.

"Yes, she's singing beautifully. I'm glad her schedule allowed her to be part of this." Augusta sipped her coffee. "Mal…something Allan Meissner said to me today concerned me." She repeated Allan's comment about feeling watched and even followed. "You know, at one time I had this odd sense of the same thing. Now I'm remembering a few times I hadn't thought about for a while, when Benjamin Rodgers was stalking me after Eugene Geller was killed a couple of years ago. I know I just thought I was imagining things then, but they turned out to be true. It's a spooky feeling." She shuddered slightly.

Another sip of coffee. "Anyway…I suggested if it continues, he might think about contacting the police. I'd think as a combat veteran he might be more alert to…well, to danger."

"What brought it up, anyway?" Mal took a last swallow of coffee.

"Nothing, really. When he walked me to my car, he looked around longer than I would have thought he needed to. But he said he didn't have any substantial reason to talk to the police."

"Do you want to relax for a while? Milly and Garrett aren't expecting us until seven." Mal stood and carried their cups and plates into the kitchen.

Augusta followed him and wrapped her arms around his slim waist from behind. *He stays so trim.* She tugged gently at his sweatshirt.

"Maybe you should change before we go to their house?"

"Are you offering to help?" He glanced back at her, a look she knew well.

"Absolutely. And maybe I'll change, too."

He turned and kissed her, a lingering kiss. "I think we both need a shower."

"That sounds perfect." Augusta almost giggled as they ran upstairs together.

Chapter Two
Reaching for Greatness

It was "Greek Night" at Milly and Garrett's, and dinner was served in the dining room on a lace tablecloth Milly had purchased in Athens. She passed around a platter of *spanakopita*—spinach pie, crispy phyllo dough filled with spinach and feta cheese—to start, as Garrett poured wine. Augusta smiled as he filled her glass with great care, thinking what a different role this was for him, the prominent defense attorney respected—and feared—by prosecuting attorneys and even some judges. With his militarily erect bearing and shock of white hair, Garrett Stoddard was an imposing figure in the courtroom.

"These are smaller than usual, but since we're making this an appetizer and there is a lot to come, I figured it would be a good idea," Milly commented. "Just remember, hearty servings of *moussak*a are coming up, so don't eat too much of this."

"How can anyone possibly eat too much s*panakopita*?" Malcolm asked, but limited himself to two slices.

Augusta sipped her wine. "Pinot noir," she guessed. "One of my favorites."

"My palette isn't refined enough for Greek wine yet," Garrett laughed. "Milly tells me this is perfectly acceptable."

Plates with the *moussaka*, a casserole of ground spiced lamb layered with eggplant and potatoes and topped with bechamel sauce, followed. A large bowl of a simple salad with greens, tomatoes, cucumbers, onion, and feta cheese was provided, with small plates for the diners to dish themselves as much as they liked.

A second platter placed on the table caused Augusta to remark with delight, "*Dolmades*! You remembered how much I love stuffed grape leaves."

"You say that every time I prepare a Greek meal," Milly said. "I don't even want to try forgetting your grape leaves."

Dinner was eaten mostly in silence, with an occasional comment: "*So* good." "This is delicious." "It's better every time you fix it."

Contented sighs, and Garrett motioned to Mal to help him clear the plates.

"I think I'm in a food coma," Augusta murmured as Milly refilled her wine glass.

"Well, don't fall asleep yet. The men are bringing dessert, and there's coffee."

Small plates of *baklava* were placed in front of the women. Milly tasted hers critically. "I think I did okay today with this. Phyllo pastry is so tricky to work with."

"It's exquisite," Augusta commented. "I doubt I'll ever attempt this. I'm afraid I'd drench it with too much honey and ruin it."

Augusta had never been much of a cook until Malcolm came into her life. Milly, a compact woman with curly, mostly silver hair, was a professionally renowned pianist on the faculty of the Conservatory. She also was a gourmet cook who loved spending time in her beautifully outfitted kitchen. Milly gave her friend some lessons in Italian cuisine, and Augusta now could make a good lasagna, among other dishes. She loved cooking for Malcolm, who appreciated that his lady had undertaken to develop a skill just for him.

They took the dishes into the kitchen before retiring to the study to enjoy their coffee.

"How was your session with Thomas Schippers?" Garrett asked Augusta. He had a vested interest: Garrett Stoddard, Esquire, was an active member of the Cincinnati Symphony Orchestra Board of Directors.

"It was delightful. What a perfect day. Thomas Schippers followed by Milly Devereaux. Or should I say Maestro Thomas Schippers followed by Master Chef Millicent Devereaux?"

The men chuckled.

"Is he as charming in a rehearsal as he is on the podium?" Milly asked.

"Absolutely, but in a different way. He projects a nice sense of 'Let's make music together' right from the beginning of the rehearsal. His enthusiasm is contagious."

Augusta sipped her coffee. "Maybe you remember the opera workshop production back in 1964 that included the 'Antonia act' of *The Tales of Hoffmann*," she continued. "Allan Meissner played Dr. Miracle then, too. And Danny's wife Martha…she was my voice student Martha Van Camp at that time…played the role of Antonia, the role she's repeating in this production. I never dreamed she would end up married to Malcolm's son. She didn't meet him until…" She turned to Malcolm. "When did Martha and Danny meet?"

Malcolm frowned, his gaze darkening. "Over a year after that production. When you were being held hostage by Nunzio Ponti. Danny was on the detail that set you free and sent Ponti to federal prison. He and Martha met then."

Oh, dear. He does NOT like to remember that time, she thought. "Yes, that's right. You know, something very good came of that…those two meeting," she added. "I remember that they seemed to be instantly attracted to each other. And now we have our wonderful grandson to enjoy."

Eager to change the subject, Augusta turned to Garrett. "Claudia Prince from the Conservatory's voice faculty is in the cast. You must know her."

"I do indeed," Garrett replied.

"She is so thrilled to be part of this production. Since so much of the act involves Antonia, Dr. Miracle, and the ghost of Antonia's mother…the role Claudia is singing in that act…that's what Thomas focused on this

26

afternoon. I filled in for Jamie and sometimes sang Hoffmann's music."

"I recently played through the music for Claudia," Milly said. "She sounds beautiful in both the roles she's performing, Giulietta in the second act and Antonia's Mother in the one you rehearsed today. What a treat for her to be performing with these singers, and especially with Jamie Logan, who did his grad work at the Conservatory right about the same time she joined the faculty. I know she'd very much like to do more performing."

"Jamie graduated in 1962, I think, and she had just joined the faculty the year before. Claudia's still in her mid-thirties. I think she'd love to do more performing. It's so difficult to build a career in opera in this country. It's very different in Europe."

"I understand Allan Meissner is a finalist in the Met Opera Auditions next month in New York," Garrett commented. "That's quite a feather in his cap. Any predictions, Augusta?"

"I encouraged him to enter, and was not at all surprised when he won at the local and regional levels."

She added thoughtfully, "You know, there are more small opera companies in the States now, since the National Endowment for the Arts has made federal money available."

"That was 1963...seven years ago," Milly interjected. "And it does seem to be making a difference."

"Yes, it does," Augusta agreed. "Another thing, a number of people in the business attend the Met auditions and sometimes offer contracts to a singer they particularly appreciate."

"So you think that might be a possibility for Allan," Mal said.

"Allan is a very gifted artist, who sings and acts unusually well. I do think that," Augusta replied.

There was quiet for a moment and Milly said, "How do you think he's doing? I mean, personally. His tour in Vietnam was a very rough time for him, I think we all know that. And it took him a while to get back on track once he got home."

"I believe he's in a much better place these days. He's worked hard to make music his life again. Dennis Halloran has been helpful, they talk often." Augusta smiled warmly as she mentioned her close friend, a Jesuit priest on the faculty of both Xavier University and Cliffside College, where she still taught two days a week. Dennis also volunteered at the VFW Post to which Allan belonged.

"What makes you think Allan is doing better?" Garrett asked.

"He seems happier. More relaxed. Reaching out to people more. It's good that he tries to help his fellow Vietnam Veterans at the VFW. When he hears what some of them have gone through…some with family members who didn't even want them to enlist…he has a better sense of perspective." She gazed at them thoughtfully. "And I hear it in his voice. He's singing with more…I don't know, more joy, maybe. More passion. He truly loves teaching, and his students adore him."

"Is he still dating that lovely woman he introduced us to at the symphony concert last month? I think she's a neighbor," Milly asked.

"Marissa Keyes," Augusta replied. "She's a professor at the University of Cincinnati, and she is indeed lovely. Single, never been married, a little older than Allan. It seemed a good match."

"Seemed?" Malcolm remarked.

"I'm sure I told all of you that Allan's commanding officer in Vietnam, Captain Leslie Jerome, moved to Cincinnati a few months ago. He and Allan have become good friends. Captain Jerome—Les—was offered a very nice position at Procter and Gamble after he retired from the military."

"Are you about to tell us the ex-Captain broke up Allan's budding romance?" Garrett grinned.

"Nothing that dramatic," Augusta laughed. "Allan was interested in Marissa, yes, but he invited Les to join them for dinner one evening and he tells me she and Leslie really clicked. He took it pretty well. Allan is focusing on getting his career off the ground. And I think he kind of liked playing matchmaker for two people he cared about."

Garrett lifted his glass. "To Allan Meissner, Cupid extraordinaire. That story convinces me more than anything you've said that he's pretty well regained his footing in civilian life."

"Well, let's hope that his challenges in this opera doesn't change that," Mal said. "Gus explained to me what a difficult role he's performing. Four distinct characters with four names. Talk about a personality disorder."

"He's *acting* the role, not *living* it," Milly reprimanded mildly.

"Don't you mean *roles*?" Garrett said. "Who are these personalities, anyway?"

"It's a unique opera," Augusta replied. "One of my favorites. The leading character, E.T.A. Hoffmann, was an actual person, a poet, musician, and painter who lived at the end of the eighteenth century and beginning of the nineteenth century. He wrote stories of fantasy, often including sinister characters who moved in and out of men's lives, sometimes tragic and even grotesque. That seems to have been what inspired Offenbach to write his opera, apparently a fascination with Hoffmann's wild flights of imagination intermingled with a vivid examination of human character and psychology. Allan has been considering the suggestion that the four villains in the opera are actually the darker side of Hoffmann himself."

Garrett lifted an eyebrow. "I hope that won't trigger some difficulties for Allan…since he is still recovering from his experiences in Vietnam. Do most bassos follow that 'darker sides of Hoffmann' theory?"

"Some do, probably more will. It's actually an intriguing idea, because each of the four villains— Lindorf, Dr. Coppelius, Dapertutto, and Dr. Miracle— manages to destroy Hoffmann's romances with four different women…each in a different way. I feel confident Allan can handle it with aplomb."

"And it's a real feather in Allan's cap to perform this role," Milly added. "This may be what firmly sets him on the path to a career. And, we all hope, eventually operatic stardom."

"An elusive goal if ever there was one," Malcolm added.

"Yet Jamie Logan has attained it, and seems to be firmly ensconced in that exalted position," Milly said. "What do you say to your ambitious students, Augusta?"

"I tell them to work like crazy, learn as much as they can, make themselves visible and watch for opportunities that open up, sometimes quite unexpectedly. I also tell them it's a tough business, and not everybody's going to make it. But some will...and it might be them."

"Sounds as if you believe Allan might be one of the lucky ones, Augusta," Garrett said.

"I certainly can't think of anyone more deserving of success."

"I hope so. He's quite a remarkable young man." Garrett replied.

***

Augusta was unusually quiet on the drive home.

"Penny for your thoughts, bride. Allan Meissner?"

"I really want this for him, Mal. He's been through so much. How wonderful if he achieved this success. Of course, it won't happen overnight. But a good performance of *The Tales of Hoffmann* with Thomas

Schippers conducting is a great start. Schippers has prestige throughout Opera World."

"So for Allan, this performance could be a case of being in the right place at the right time, and impressing the right person." They had passed Hyde Park Square, and Mal turned off Madison Road and headed for their house on Vista Circle.

"If he performs as well as I know he can, yes, it definitely could be that." She sighed. "And as I said, Allan is so deserving of a break."

She was silent for a moment. "I see greatness in him, Mal. Not just as a singer, but as an inspiration for others."

Chapter Thee
An Unexpected Event

Friday, March 6, 1970
8:30 a.m.

After taking Fritz for a walk around her pleasant neighborhood in the brisk late winter air, Augusta sat at the desk in her special room on the second floor. In the combination office and exercise room she used the ballet barre daily for at least a half hour. A desk, bookcase and cabinet sat in one corner for her to handle scheduling and other paperwork.

Lifting her leg onto the barre, she examined herself critically in the mirror. *No gray showing in my hair yet, I can wait until next week for my hair appointment.* She knew she was vain, but liked that she looked considerably younger than her age, and she worked hard to keep her trim figure. Her hairdresser kept the gray away with a shade of chestnut she liked, and seldom varied her medium bob. Good genes meant no obvious wrinkles—yet.

Milly, whose curly hair was at this point almost completely silver, chided Augusta from time to time. "Good grief, Augusta, you're a grandmother, for heaven's sake. Your little Maxie doesn't care if you look older than forty." But the comments were made in good humor. The women had known each other for decades, since they were freshmen together at the Conservatory. After graduation they lived together in Europe for three years, mostly in Paris. When Milly's marriage to a doctor at New York's Mount Sinai Hospital fell apart, she moved to be with family in California. Augusta had been thrilled when her friend returned to Cincinnati in 1960 to join the Conservatory staff.

Augusta glanced over her schedule of rehearsals for *The Tales of Hoffmann.* Since she had included students at the Conservatory and local people who were regulars in the Summer Opera Chorus, she had some flexibility in how she handled the schedule. The production would be performed twice the weekend of March 20 and 21—only two weeks away. The chorus had already met for musical rehearsals, and Maestro Schippers had made time in his extremely busy schedule to work with the soloists at different times.

Augusta would meet with the singers for four rehearsals, one act at a time, to give them her staging directions. Following those rehearsals was the *sitzprobe,* the rehearsal with singers and orchestra to integrate the musical elements of the opera. The singers would be seated or standing, the focus being strictly on the music.

This would be Maestro Schippers' rehearsal, though Augusta would attend and make notes of any possible changes she might need to make with the staging.

On her schedule she had marked the four staged rehearsals during the next week, and two dress rehearsals on the Monday and Wednesday before the performances. Augusta felt a flutter in her chest as she stared at those dates. *This is actually happening. It's exciting but a little scary. My debut as a professional opera stage director. Let's pray everybody stays healthy.*

She placed the papers in her briefcase, went into her bedroom and selected her dress for the day. Augusta loved clothes and could wear anything due to her tall, slender figure. Another vanity, she knew, but she had a closet filled with fashionable items, and the back of the door held numerous pairs of her beloved stiletto shoes.

She eyed a new outfit she'd just picked up. Augusta wasn't sure about the newer fashions which echoed what hippies were wearing or the colorful new disco look, but this one she had thought she could handle. A sleeveless sage green Italian knit dress with an A-line skirt.

Turning one way and then the other in the mirror, she thought, *Not bad. Okay, but I'm not giving up my stiletto heels—no go-go boots or platforms for me.* Putting the finishing touches on her make-up, Augusta glanced at the framed picture of Malcolm and her on their wedding day, five years ago.

She loved this picture, because Mal so often projected a serious, even stern visage, and in this photo his happiness was reflected in what she thought of as his "thousand-watt smile." When they first crossed paths at a crime scene there had been considerable friction between them, but their relationship blossomed as she helped him solve the case. Over the following years she had assisted with other cases, sometimes overstepping and finding herself in precarious positions. Each time, Malcolm had come to her rescue.

Another photo of their whole family. Mal and Augusta in the center with Mal's attorney son Ryan and his wife Lacey, an accomplished actress with the Parkside Playhouse, on their left. On their right, Mal's younger son Danny, who had followed in his father's footsteps and was a police detective, with wife Martha and their adorable three-year-old son, named Malcolm after his grandfather but called "Maxie." So, while in her mid-fifties, Augusta had become the matriarch of a family, something she had never expected. She wore the title proudly and adored her new family.

Thinking happy thoughts, Augusta picked up her briefcase, preparing to leave for the Conservatory and begin her Friday morning voice lessons. The sudden ringing of the telephone was jarring, and she felt apprehensive as she picked it up.

Malcolm's voice, his official Chief-of-Detectives tone. "Gus, I have some bad news. You may want to sit down for this."

She sank onto the chaise next to their bed. "What's going on, Mal?"

"I heard from a detective in the Sheriff's Office that Leslie Jerome was found dead in his Elmwood Place apartment this morning. Two shots to the heart."

"Dear God!" Augusta clutched her stomach.

"You know the Village of Elmwood Place has their own police department. They aren't equipped to deal with this, so the Hamilton County Sheriff's Department is handling the investigation. Herb…Lieutenant Vogel…is in charge."

"Oh, Malcolm. How awful. Allan will be devastated. He and Leslie had become such close friends."

"I thought you might want to call Allan and let him know before he hears it on the news somewhere. It will be at least on the noon news, and of course in all the papers."

"I'll probably see him when I get to the Conservatory; I'm on my way now," Augusta said. *We're supposed to have a rehearsal tomorrow. I may need to reschedule it.* She shook off the thought. *For heavens' sake, Augusta, at this moment that's such a minor part of Allan's life. A man he liked and admired survived Vietnam, only to be shot to death in his own home.*

"Does he get there early? It would be good if you could tell him in person. This news will be difficult for him."

"To say the least," she agreed. "Yes, he usually arrives about the same time I do, and he often comes to my studio and we spend some time talking. And I'd much rather tell him in person."

"I can't tell you how much I regretted having to make this call to you," Malcolm said. "The detective who called me was aware you were friendly with Allan Meissner, and they had learned Meissner was someone who was friends with Jerome."

"How did they know that?"

"That I don't know yet, but I'll find out. This is going to be very tough for Allan to deal with," he repeated.

"I'll talk to him, and suggest he go to see Dennis. The good priest has been helpful to Allan in the past." A sudden thought. "And, oh … maybe we should contact Leslie's girlfriend Marissa? From what Allan's told me, she and Leslie are…*were*…getting quite serious."

"Absolutely not. Because of their relationship, she will be interviewed and investigated by the Sheriff's Office before she can be eliminated as a suspect in the murder. You could be regarded as interfering with Vogel's investigation by alerting her to the situation."

Augusta drove directly to the Conservatory, parked, went to her studio to find Allan waiting at her door, smiling. *Oh Allan, I'm about to destroy your day. And many days to come.*

His smile faded as he sensed her distress. "Something wrong, Augusta?"

"Please come in." She unlocked the door, motioned for him to have a seat, and sat down in a chair she pulled closer to his. "I have something I have to tell you, and I would give the world if I didn't need to do this."

He gazed at her, alarmed.

A deep breath. *Just say it.* "Malcolm called me just as I was leaving. It's Leslie Jerome."

"Something's happened to him." A pause. "Something bad."

"Allan...," she laid a hand on his arm. "Leslie's dead. This morning he was found shot to death in his apartment."

Allan stared at her as if trying to comprehend what she had just said. She rested her other hand on his shoulder.

A range of emotions crossed his face as he gripped the hand she had rested on his arm.

"Scream, cry, let it out. This must be unbelievably awful news to hear." Allan's eyes filled with tears.

"Not Les...not Captain Jerome. One of the best people I've ever known." A heart-wrenching sob suddenly escaped him, and Augusta wrapped her arms around him, holding him for long moments.

He sat up abruptly. "Who the hell did this?"

"We don't know yet. The Cincinnati Police Department doesn't have jurisdiction in Elmwood Place. The case has been turned over to the Hamilton County Sheriff, and one of the detectives called Malcolm because he was aware Malcolm might know Leslie."

"Marissa. Somebody has to let her know." He stood and went to Augusta's desk, picking up the phone, stared at it and reseated the handset. "I can't do this."

"It's very possible she's been contacted. I'm sure the detectives are interviewing Leslie's neighbors...and it's likely some of them have met Marissa."

"Augusta, I was there just last night. I took Les a recording of *Hoffmann*...he was fine."

Augusta didn't comment, but felt a flicker of fear. *Oh, dear. I'm sorry he did that, but how would he know what was coming?*

"I should go to see Marissa. She must be devastated."

Alarm bells sounded in the back of Augusta's brain. "Don't do anything yet, Allan. Let me talk to Mal and share with him what you just told me."

"You mean about being at Les's apartment last night?" A stricken look. "We talked. We had coffee. I told him some things about the opera. He was looking forward to seeing it." More tears gathered in his eyes. "He and Marissa had bought tickets."

They were silent for a moment. "Allan...we have a staging rehearsal tomorrow morning. I can reschedule it, if that would be better. It's just for the Prologue, so it won't be long. I could combine it with the Act One rehearsal."

Allan stared at his feet. "No, I'd rather be in rehearsal than sitting around grieving for Les and wondering who the hell shot him to death." He stared into her eyes. "Who could have done this? Why would they have done it? Les was one of the best guys I've ever known. It doesn't make any sense. Could it have been some kind of random...maybe a robbery gone bad?"

"Hopefully, they'll solve it quickly," Augusta said. Neither of them had spoken aloud what she was thinking, and she wondered if it had crossed Allan's mind, that he could be a suspect. *I have to call Mal immediately, and ask how Allan should volunteer the information about having been at Leslie's apartment last night. He may have been the last person to see him alive before someone broke in and killed him.*

40

Allan stood. "I need to go to the office and cancel my lessons for the day. Then I may go to see Marissa."

"Allan, I think you should go see Dennis Halloran immediately, before you do anything else. I need to talk to Malcolm and then I'll call you." She thought for a moment. "He will most likely say you should call the Sheriff's Office. That you were there last night before the murder would be very important information. Malcolm will know who to call."

She picked up her briefcase. "I'm cancelling today's lessons as well. I know I won't be much good to my students today."

They gazed at each other again, Augusta acutely aware of the pain in Allan's face, the lost look in his eyes. She hugged him tightly.

Chapter Four
A City of Music

Saturday, March 7, 1970
10:00 a.m.

No matter how many times she entered Cincinnati's Music Hall and no matter the reason, Augusta never ceased to feel this beautiful, iconic building was a sacred place, a place created by music, for music.

The many German immigrants who gravitated to the "Queen City of the West" brought with them the tradition of group singing, and eventually some choirs began to join together to hold festivals. Eventually, a *Saengerbund*—a choral society—of some two thousand voices assembled. In 1873 the first May Music Festival was held, and the large wooden building constructed for these festivals proving inadequate, the incredible Victorian Gothic Revival structure she now entered first opened its doors in 1878. How many performances, festivals, trade shows, political events, and other such gatherings had it hosted?

She had talked about Music Hall with Thomas Schippers at their first rehearsal together, and he echoed her thoughts. "You know, this building literally takes my breath away every time I see it. What a remarkable history it has and what glorious events it continues to bring to this city. It's one reason I accepted this post. This is a city rich in tradition that appreciates music as few do."

"I felt that from the time I started school here at the Conservatory, decades ago. I'm a Philadelphian by birth and upbringing…but Cincinnati is my city. A city of music."

"A kindred spirit," Schippers smiled. "I'm not surprised to learn this about you."

At the rehearsal this morning, however, he would not be present. Augusta's task today was to work with part of the cast to teach basic staging; Maestro Schippers had assigned a staff accompanist to play for them. Augusta went into the auditorium, glancing at the beautiful new chandelier hanging from the ceiling that her dear friend Tobias Dietrich had helped provide for this hall. Augusta still found it difficult to process that Tobias had recently left this life. *I lost a great friend. Thank you for everything, dear Tobias.*

Using her cast list, Augusta checked off names as singers arrived. She liked hearing their warm greetings as well as introductions. Everyone was happy to be in this production.

Soon everyone had arrived for the rehearsal…except Allan Meissner. Augusta checked her watch. *Allan is never late; what could have happened?*

The cast was enjoying their time getting acquainted, so she took a moment to run to the lobby and attempted to reach him on his phone. After the phone rang eight times she replaced the handset; hopefully, that meant Allan was on his way. She returned to the auditorium, rapping a music stand for attention.

"I have no idea what's holding Allan Meissner up, but let's get started. We can work his aria in later."

To her delight, her cast had been scheduled to be on the main stage in Music Hall for this rehearsal. They would be setting the staging for the Prologue of *The Tales of Hoffmann.* A relatively short act, the cast for this scene included the men in the chorus portraying students; the characters of Hoffmann, Lindorf, and the mezzo-soprano playing the dual role of The Muse of Poetry and Hoffmann's companion, Nicklausse. Since the opera included spoken dialogue the Summer Opera opted to perform it in English, which Augusta thought was a good choice.

Irene Madison, another Conservatory graduate who was enjoying a busy career mostly in Europe, had made the two weeks of preparation for this production part of her schedule and Augusta was very happy she was in attendance. Augusta thought Irene's voice, appearance, and fine acting ability were perfect for the role of the Muse. She was a good friend of Jamie Logan's and she had happily accepted Augusta's invitation to be part of this cast. Augusta smiled as she watched Irene bonding with the men in the chorus, who obviously appreciated her warmth and friendliness.

A current graduate student of Augusta's, tenor George Van Dorn, was in the chorus. George had volunteered to be Jamie's stand-in for staging rehearsals, eager to have an opportunity to begin work on the role for his own future repertoire. Augusta accepted the offer, reminding herself the talented but once lazy George had developed the desire and discipline to possibly make his dream come true. He was one of the students she was thinking of at Milly's recent dinner party with her comment that "someone is going to make it, and it might be you."

Since the act began with a spoken monologue from the Muse, Augusta motioned to George, fishing change from her purse. "Will you try to call Allan again? Here's the number. Since Lindorf doesn't interact much in the Prologue we can manage without him, but I'm getting a little concerned. Allan is never late."

George nodded and left the stage, returning a short time later as Irene completed her scene. He mouthed "no answer" to Augusta and joined the other male choristers.

Augusta skipped over Lindorf's entrance and brief dialogue exchange with another character, and his short aria. She positioned the chorus men, asking them to bring chairs on stage and pretend they were sitting around tables. It was amusing to see them swirling beer in non-existent steins, leaning on the invisible tables.

George, music score in hand, then entered in the role of Hoffmann, accompanied by Nicklausse—Irene's "alter ego" role—and the jovial atmosphere of the students continued to be projected. Augusta had asked them to remember this was a party in a bar, and they were happy to provide her with that. She was pleased that they didn't overdo it; some of these men were professional choristers, and the Conservatory students wisely took their cue from the more experienced singers. Observing her multi-ethnic chorus pleased Augusta even more. A few years ago that wouldn't have been the case.

Watching Irene as Nicklausse comfortably joining the party, Augusta found it intriguing that the composer, Offenbach, once again cast a character in multiple roles, or rather, dual roles in this instance. Banter among the students, as they persuaded Hoffmann to tell them the legend of a disabled dwarf named Kleinzach. During the aria, the music changed as Hoffmann's mind wandered and he sang of women he has loved. George performed the aria well, marking the score with Augusta's stage directions. He seemed startled when he received a generous round of applause from the male choristers. The students then urged Hoffmann to tell them the story of the women he had mentioned, and the prologue ended with Hoffmann responding, "The name of the first was Olympia."

Still no Allan. Augusta became somewhat alarmed, concerned he might have had an accident on his way to rehearsal. She thanked her cast and the Music Hall staff accompanist warmly and dismissed them, gathering up materials and placing them in her briefcase. To her considerable surprise, Father Dennis Halloran met her in the lobby.

"Dennis?"

"Hold onto your hat, Augusta. I'm afraid I have more bad news. Allan's been arrested and may be charged with the murder of Leslie Jerome."

A shocked Augusta stared at Dennis, nearly dropping her briefcase as her knees buckled. "*What*?"

Dennis placed a hand under her elbow to steady her. "He called me earlier and asked me to let you know. He was stopped by a CPD patrol car not long after he drove away from his apartment. They claimed he'd run a stop sign and had him get out of his car. A search turned up a pistol, and the gun is now being examined to see if the bullets match the ones that killed Leslie."

"Dear God, Dennis."

"I've already been in touch with Garrett Stoddard, and he's on his way to the courthouse. In fact, he may be there by now." He took her briefcase as they moved toward the main exit to the building.

"I'm parked right outside. Garrett said he'd arrange for you to have a brief visit with Allan. I'll drive you there."

She nodded. "We talked last night. He spent a little time with Marissa Keyes yesterday before her parents arrived to be here with her. He also told me he called the Sheriff's Office to let them know he'd been at Leslie's Thursday night for about an hour and a half. How could they possibly have suspected him? Just because he was there? He and Leslie were close friends. How did Allan sound on the phone, Dennis?"

"Strangely, quite subdued…in a state of shock, I can well imagine."

Augusta slid into the front passenger seat of Dennis' Volkswagen. He handed her the briefcase and moved to the other side, ducking his head as he took the driver's seat. *Why on earth would a man as tall as Dennis buy a little VW?* She swallowed a laugh; it was the result of nerves, she was sure. Augusta took deep breaths to steady herself and said very little during the brief drive into downtown Cincinnati.

Chapter Five
"To Ward Off All Danger"

They arrived at the Hamilton County Courthouse within moments. Another imposing, iconic building in Augusta's city, but one with a very different purpose. Designed with clean Renaissance Revival lines, it occupied a full block in the downtown area, housing the courts, sheriff, prosecutor, clerk of courts, and other offices. She knew Allan would be held in the county jail on the sixth floor of the building.

Dennis waited in a small vestibule inside the first floor entrance as Augusta was allowed a short visit. An elevator took her up to the jail. Seeing Allan in a cell increased her nerves, and she tried hard to conceal them from her friend.

"I apologize, Augusta. I wish I'd been able to let you know why I couldn't make the rehearsal this morning." He still seemed surprisingly calm. "You know it's likely I'm going to be charged with Leslie's murder."

"Garrett is on his way here," Augusta told him. "This is preposterous. Why on earth would they charge you with this?"

"They searched my car, did Dennis tell you that? They found a semiautomatic pistol with a suppressor. The bullets that killed Captain Howard are the kind for the gun found in my car." He ran his hand over the back of his head.

"Suppressor?"

"Silencer. And it's military issue. Augusta, I don't even own a gun. I didn't buy one here, and I didn't buy one in Baltimore. And I sure as hell didn't bring one home with me from Vietnam. I had enough of guns while I was there." He sat down abruptly, suddenly looking vulnerable and somehow smaller. "I don't understand what's happening, any of this…how did that gun end up in my car?"

Augusta leaned against the bars, wishing she could hug Allan. "Garrett will work all of this out. Why on earth do they think you would have called the Sheriff's Office and volunteered the information you were at Leslie's last night if you'd…if you'd shot him? That alone doesn't make any sense."

"Not to you. Malcolm might be able to answer that question."

She stared at him. "I need to call him." She paused a moment and then added, "Garrett is absolutely the best. He'll get you out of here, I guarantee it."

A guard interrupted them. "Mrs. Mitchell, you have to leave. Sir, your attorney is here. I'll take you to the interview room."

Well, at least he called him 'sir.' "I'll wait downstairs, Allan. Dennis is still here."

Augusta was relieved to see Malcolm and Dennis standing next to Dennis' car, talking. Malcolm wrapped his arms around her and held her for a long moment.

"You're shivering, Gus. It's chilly. Let's all wait in the car," Malcolm said.

Once they were inside, Augusta asked how Malcolm had learned about Allan's arrest. "Dennis called me," he responded. "How's Allan?"

"Handling this remarkably well," she replied. She turned to Dennis. "Have you had a chance to see him?"

"No, not yet. We had a good talk last night, though. He's come a long way in the past few months, but Leslie's death is difficult for him. And he's very concerned about Marissa."

She glanced from one man to the other. "Garrett's here now. Did you see him come in?"

"Yes, but he headed upstairs immediately. Rightly so." Malcolm leaned forward. "I've picked up some information, but let's see what Garrett has to say. I'm sure he'll find a way to get Allan out on bail."

"Well, that will probably take a while," Dennis said. He looked across the street. "Why don't we go over to Frisch's and get coffee and something to eat?"

"That sounds like an excellent plan." Malcolm opened the door for Augusta as he added, "My treat."

Augusta seldom ate the food from Frisch's Big Boy, but was surprised to find she was starving. "Brawny Lad and onion rings, please. And a coke."

"I'll have what she's having," Dennis said with a slight smile.

Mal chuckled. "You must be hungry, Gus."

"Nerves," she replied. Mal ordered coffee, a Big Boy, onion rings, and chili.

"So what can you tell us?" Augusta asked Mal, once the waitress left.

"The Sheriff's Office had an anonymous phone call at some point. The caller claimed the murder weapon could be found in Allan's car. It was confirmed that Allan had called the office and told them he'd visited Leslie Jerome last night. And a neighbor told them she'd seen a man she recognized as Allan come into the building around seven-thirty or so. She also claimed to have heard loud voices coming from Leslie's apartment sometime during the next hour. She didn't see Allan leave."

"She sounds like the kind of neighbor people try to avoid," Augusta said.

"It was enough for them to decide they needed to find a way to check out his car. If there was no gun, no harm done."

"So, that stop for Allan supposedly committing a traffic violation was probably a ruse," Augusta said. "But there was a gun. And apparently, the bullets that killed Leslie came from that gun." Augusta pressed her hands to her forehead. "What a nightmare."

"No fingerprints on the gun, by the way. But there's more," Mal said. "Talk about a nosy neighbor. She told them she believed Leslie Jerome and Allan Meissner were both involved with the same woman."

"So they think they have motive," Dennis commented. "A love triangle."

Their food arrived, and Augusta waited as Dennis said a silent grace before replying. "Nonsense. Marissa will disabuse them of that misunderstanding quickly. The three of them were all good friends."

"Eventually, Garrett will know everything the cops know. They're required by law to share any and all evidence with him." He gazed directly at her. "You won't like hearing this, but at some point, they'll search Allan's apartment. And maybe his studio at the Conservatory."

A sudden thought, the title of an aria of Allan's in the opera: *Pour conjurer le danger—To ward off all danger.* Augusta sighed. "This is awful. Things have been going so well for Allan recently. He seemed to be well on his way to truly establishing a career. And now this. My heart breaks for him."

"Don't borrow trouble, Gus," Mal said. "Let's see what Garrett finds out."

"What will he have to do to get Allan out of there?" Dennis asked, waving a hand toward the courthouse.

"Since it's the weekend, his arraignment will probably be sometime Monday morning. My guess is Garrett will get in touch with Judge Demarest and ask him to set bond now. After that, Allan can be released." Malcolm finished his last bite of chili. "Bond will be high because it's a murder case. That may be a serious problem."

"No, it isn't," Augusta replied immediately. "I have a trust fund. Garrett has money. Milly has an expensive house. No matter how much it is, we can handle it."

"You think Milly would use her house as collateral?" Mal sounded skeptical.

"All of us...including you, I know...will do whatever is necessary for Allan. We all know he is not capable of murdering anyone."

Mal leaned back. "He killed people in Vietnam, Gus."

"Totally different. He hated doing it. You know that. It was war. To shoot to death a person he loved? Impossible. He's a creative artist. He was a warrior for a brief period, but he's trying hard to put that behind him...and he's succeeding."

Mal nodded. "I realize how different what he experienced in Vietnam was from my time with the Marines in the Second World War. He's had a tough time of it."

They finished their food and sat quietly for a moment, each lost in their thoughts.

Garrett finally came through the courthouse door and Dennis ran outside and waved to him to join them.

"Allan can be released now, so I'll make this quick." Garrett sighed. "The gun was a match for the bullets recovered from Captain Jerome's body. Allan has been formally arrested and charged. I was able to convince Judge Demarest to set bond now, so I called Milly and shes's on her way. She's willing to put up her house but it won't be enough. We still need about a hundred and fifty thousand dollars."

"I can take care of that," Augusta said firmly. It was half the money in her trust.

"We'll split it." Garrett said. "Excellent. Once the bond has been taken care of, I'll take Allan to our house. He'll be formally arraigned Monday morning at the courthouse. But for now, he's out of here, and we can discuss our strategy going forward. This is serious stuff, folks."

"Allan said something to me…about how did that gun get into his car?" Augusta said. She stared at Malcolm. "Obviously someone planted it. Broke into his car and put it there. But who would do that? And why?"

Chapter Six
An Incident in Vietnam

As Allan came through the doors of the courthouse, he stared at the line-up of people waiting to greet him. Augusta reached for him and gave him a long embrace. Dennis gripped his friend's shoulder.

"Thanks so much for everything," he said. "This means a lot, all your support and help." Stepping back, he gazed at Garrett. "What happens now?"

"We pick up your car from impound. Don't worry about the fees, I'll cover them for now and you can pay me back when it's convenient. Then we'll go to your apartment so you can pick up whatever you need. You're my and Milly's house guest for the present, until we get this straightened out," Garrett said.

"I keep hoping I'm going to wake up," Allan ran a hand over the back of his head, a familiar gesture. "This is all totally unreal."

"Sorry to say, it's very real," Malcolm told him. "There's not a strong case, but having the murder weapon in your possession is enough for law enforcement to pursue a trial."

"It wasn't in my possession. It was in the trunk of my car. And my fingerprints weren't on it."

"It's not difficult to wipe a gun clean of everything," Garrett said. "This is a big case, and Herb Vogel is now handling it. What a feather in his cap if he could win this."

"He won't," Augusta said. "We all know that."

Garrett took Allan's elbow. "My car's down the street a bit." He nodded toward his friends as he and Allan moved away. "Why don't you meet us at Milly's? We need to pursue Augusta's thought—which I'm sure has crossed all our minds—that the gun was planted in Allan's car. There's no other plausible explanation."

"Speaking of cars, I need to go back to Music Hall and get mine," Augusta said.

Dennis offered to drive her back to Music Hall, and Augusta and Mal would then meet at home and head for Milly's. It had been overcast, but the sun began to break through the clouds as they drove.

"Nice to see the sun," Dennis commented.

"I'll take it as a good omen," Augusta remarked. "Allan will make it through this, just as he made it through Vietnam. But Dennis…how much can one man take?"

"Who would want Allan accused and convicted of the crime of murder? He's a good man, Augusta. I have a difficult time imagining how this is happening to him."

On her drive home, Augusta turned that thought over in her mind. *Who would do this to Allan? Since I first met him as a freshman all those years ago, he's always been a generous, kind person, well-liked by everyone at the Conservatory. I met his parents before his father died, and they were so proud of him. As much because of his character as his obvious talent. This is so unfair.*

***

Malcolm and Fritz were just returning to the house after a short walk as Augusta turned into their driveway. Fritz pulled on his leash, tail wagging furiously, as he strained to greet her. Mal moved closer and Augusta bent to hug her sweet dog. She had given Fritz to Malcolm as an early birthday present nearly five years earlier, and he soon became an important part of their lives. Augusta had never owned a puppy until Fritz. It had a been a learning experience that required not only training Fritz, but also realizing she had a lot to learn about being a dog "mommy." Now she couldn't imagine life without him.

After settling Fritz, Augusta and Mal both changed into casual clothing. Augusta glanced at her rugged husband as he undressed, admiring his muscular torso as her eyes sought out the scars from bullet wounds. One in his abdomen, barely visible. A wound that had kept him away from his job for months, and the event that convinced his ex-wife Carla she did not want to be married to a cop, despite the two young sons they shared. Another on his right shoulder, more recent. And a third on his left shoulder from the previous year. That one

Augusta had nursed him through. He sat on the edge of the bed and pulled her down beside him.

"Inventorying my battle scars. I always know when you're doing that." He kissed her softly.

"The ones I know about." She took his left hand, tracing a long scar across his palm. "This knife wound bled so much. I was so scared that might be the end of your career."

"But it wasn't. I'm tough as nails, Gus. You know that. What made you do the inventory today?"

"I'm thinking about the scars that don't show. The mental scars. Close calls. Allan managed to avoid being wounded in Vietnam, but he bears psychological scars from things that happened while he was there. It will be a long time before those heal."

She leaned back and gazed into his face. "And now this. Being arrested for a murder he didn't commit...and the victim was his commanding officer in Vietnam. Allan's not being allowed the time to mourn his friend."

"You can imagine how frustrating this is for me," Malcom responded. "I can't even appear to be interfering in the sheriff's case. Why couldn't this have happened in my jurisdiction? The CPD would be looking for the real killer and Allan would be mourning his friend's death in peace."

He pulled Augusta to her feet. "We need to get to Milly's so we can start building our strategy for Allan's defense."

***

Allan ate hungrily from the casserole Milly had placed on the table, talking between bites and sometimes even during a bite. It was late afternoon, so Milly had prepared food for all of them to help themselves to whenever they liked.

"You know, I had a happy childhood," Allan said. "Pretty normal. No siblings, but lots of friends. A neighborhood boys' gang that hung out and did all the kid stuff. Riding bikes, playing baseball, football…well, our version of those sports, anyway. Junior high was when I started to grow like crazy. I added six inches in seventh grade and decided to play basketball when I got to high school. I was six feet four as a freshman and grew another inch and a half during those years."

"Did you ever have anyone comment about your height in an uncomplimentary way?" Garrett asked. "Kids can sometimes be mean about someone who looks different."

"I got teased more about being serious about my singing than I did about my height. Being on the basketball team made it okay for me to be extra tall, because I helped win a lot of games for my school." Allan chuckled at the memory. "I played center and regularly took that ball away from our opponents." Another large bite of casserole. "This is delicious. I didn't realize how hungry I was."

"And you dated in high school?" Dennis asked. "Tall girls, I would guess."

"No, I actually liked little girls. And they liked me. Maybe because my mom is short." His eyes widened. "My mother. Oh, my God, I need to call her." He glanced around the table. "How do you tell your mother...," his voice trailed off.

"That will wait until tomorrow, Allan," Dennis said. "We can call her together."

"Thank you. I can't deal with that right now. She thinks the world of you, Father Dennis."

The expression of relief mixed with the pain on Allan's face brought tears to Augusta's eyes. She'd met Allan's lovely mother Maureen and knew how much she loved and supported her son. *Maureen is an exceptional woman. She'll probably want to jump on the next plane and fly up here...and maybe she should.*

Allan took a gulp of iced tea and set his jaw. "We're trying to figure out who might have framed me. Can we just stick with that for now?"

Malcom leaned forward, going into 'full detective mode,' as Augusta thought of it. "Let's start with high school. No one that you had a run-in with that might have turned into a life-long grudge?"

"No, that never happened. I had good teen years. Better than most people, I think. Sometimes they'd call me 'Mario Lanza' because of my singing, but I'd set them straight by reminding them Lanza was a tenor, and I'm a bass. It was all pretty good-natured. Maybe they respected me because along with being tall, I was strong as an ox and they'd have been on the wrong side in a fist fight."

"Augusta has already spoken to how well-liked you were at the Conservatory," Malcom said, and Allan nodded. "Why did you volunteer for the military after the Vietnam War started?"

"I love my country," Allan said. "And my dad served in the Marines in World War II. My mom had a brother who served in Korea. I think I did it partly from respect for that tradition in both my parents' families. I wanted to do my part."

Allan leaned back in his chair, his fingers locked behind his head. "Vietnam was...difficult. Not at all what I'd expected from the war stories I'd heard from my dad and my uncle." A frown. "Things happened over there that were...well, ugly. Sometimes even wrong."

"So different from World War II," Mal said. "We knew what we were fighting for, who the enemy was. Vietnam isn't even a war—it's a 'police action."

Allan nodded and sighed, reaching for his glass and taking another drink of tea. "I try not to think about this, but I can't forget it." He looked off into the distance, his dark eyes troubled.

"One time...I was out on patrol with some of the men from my division, and something...I know you've heard about the booby traps. The Viet Cong would plant explosives on the jungle floor and wire them together, then hide a wire that would set them off if it was accidentally tripped. One of our men stepped on the wire and...." he glanced at the women. "This isn't easy to tell with ladies in the room."

"We've heard these stories, Allan," Milly assured him. "They're difficult to hear, and they must be even harder to tell. Please go ahead."

"The only way to tell it is how I remember it. Bodies flew in all directions. Most of us were able to jump off the path. But…three of our men were killed. Two others were wounded."

The room grew totally silent.

"We gathered up the dead and wounded and tried to pull ourselves together and head back toward our base. To get there we had to go through a Vietnamese village." He took a deep breath. "Here's the thing…we never really knew who were friends and who were enemies. Viet Cong, or working for the Viet Cong. When we entered the village, our sergeant completely lost his cool…he was enraged."

Another deep breath, as Allan relived his experience. "He took his rifle and started beating some of the old men with its butt. I mean, hitting them as hard as he could. Even a couple of the young boys. None of us knew what we should do. Some of us begged him to stop, but he was…beyond hearing us. Every one of the Vietnamese villagers was screaming and crying, some of the women herding their children into the jungle to get away from him. He even shot an old guy who was trying to protect his grandchildren."

"Mother of Mercy," Dennis said softly.

Allan sighed deeply and sat up straighter. "We finally physically restrained him. When we let him go, he acted like nothing had happened and ordered us to continue back to base. None of us said anything to each other, that was a silent march. But I couldn't keep silent; I went to our captain…as you know, that was Leslie Jerome. I felt compelled to report what had happened. I didn't really want to continue serving under that sergeant and see that happen again, so I asked my captain if I could be transferred."

"And were you?" Mal asked.

"No, instead Les reported it to our commanding officer, and the sergeant was disciplined. Severely. It took a little time, but we learned that he was court-martialed and sentenced to a year at Long Binh Jail, there in Vietnam. We had a new sergeant who was a great guy."

"Sounds somewhat like the situation we learned about recently at the village of My Lai," Garrett commented.

Allan nodded. "That wasn't the only time something similar happened. There were other such occurrences. I learned later that sergeant also spent time in Leavenworth for other offenses and was dishonorably discharged. One of the guys in my unit went to see him...trying to do a nice thing, I guess. He found out Sergeant Bridges had hoped to build a career in the military, and of course what happened ended that. He told me Bridges swore that Captain Jerome and I would regret having reported him, if it was the last thing he ever did."

Augusta said, "Did you say the sergeant's name was Bridges?"

"Yes. Luke Bridges."

"Do you know where he was from?" Augusta reached for Malcolm's hand and clutched it.

"Yeah. Las Vegas." He glanced around the room. "It's too bad what happened to him...but he brought it on himself. He figured nobody in the unit would have the guts to report him, I think, because all of us were afraid of him. Apparently, he really hated me for reporting it."

Again, the room fell silent. "It's possible he still hates you, Allan," Garrett said. "It sounds as if he may blame you for ruining his life."

Chapter Seven
Sin City and the Ponti Family

"It's not an uncommon name, but there was a Bridges family over in Newport, Kentucky, that we had some dealings with," Augusta mused. "They left Newport and moved to Las Vegas several years ago."

"Yes, the Bridges were one of a number of families now living in Vegas who moved there from Newport," Garrett said.

Allan glanced from Augusta to Garrett. "As Augusta said, it's a common name. I don't know what this has to do with the guy I just told you about."

"Hearing the name Bridges always puts us on alert," Malcolm explained, "because of our experiences with them. The Newport Bridges are a branch of a Mafia family from New York, the Pontis, who moved to Las Vegas as well. The head of that family is a man named Nunzio Ponti, who is now serving time in a federal prison. The Newport family branch had changed their name to Bridges."

"I get it—Ponti means 'bridges' in Italian," Allan said.

"You may not have been aware of the unsavory reputation of Newport," Mal continued. "Chances are you were never over there while you were in undergrad school, and it's been pretty well cleaned up in the past few years. But there was a long stretch where the folks from Cincinnati who were looking for certain illicit activities just had to drive across the Ohio River to find whatever they wanted. We had our own 'Sin City' right across the river."

"Oh, I heard about it, I just never had any urge to gamble...or whatever else people went to Newport for."

Augusta leaned toward Allan. "Do you remember Bobby Bridges?"

"Sure I do. He was in my class. A very fine tenor, one of your students. I recall he didn't graduate with me...in fact, I think he dropped out of school right at the start of our senior year. That was too bad."

"Well...it turned out Bobby was a member of the Newport crime family."

Allan snapped his fingers. "Wait a minute...Bobby had a crush on Martha, your daughter-in-law. She was Martha Van Camp back then and in the grad program. I remember he hung around the school even after he'd dropped out, and she wasn't too happy about that."

He stood and walked to the window, leaning back on the sill. "Something happened the weekend of our opera workshop production, and after that Bobby never showed up again."

"Yes, there was an…incident." Augusta glanced at Mal, wondering how much she should say. They'd kept the situation as quiet as they could, but there had been a mention in the newspapers about a member of Nunzio Ponti's family being in hiding for fear his life was in danger.

"A couple of guys got arrested because they were trying to kidnap Augusta," Allan continued. "I'd almost forgotten about that."

Mal hid a smile as he cleared his throat, and Augusta relaxed. *I need to remember what a small town Cincinnati can be, no matter how many people live here. Word gets around.*

Garrett came to their rescue. "Bobby went into the witness protection program because he helped save Augusta from being kidnapped, probably the best thing he ever did in his entire life. But because he was in danger of retaliation from the Pontis, he was given a new name and sent out west."

"But he came back to see Martha the next time we had a situation with the Pontis," Augusta said. "He could have gotten himself killed. He's back in WITSEC—the federal witness security program—now, and if he has any sense at all, he'll stay there."

"Wow. It sounds like the Ponti-Bridges crew are good people to stay away from," Allan remarked. "And you're wondering if Luke Bridges is one of them."

"I think it's worth investigating. Your friend who went to see Luke Bridges at Leavenworth, he saw him in the prison in Kansas, correct?" Mal asked, and Allan nodded. "What else do you remember him saying about

71

that? Maybe what Bridges' plans were when he was released?"

"It wasn't long before Luke was due to be released, and if I remember right, he planned to go home to Las Vegas. He said Luke told him he had a lot of family there and he'd try to figure out where he could get a job and get on his feet. He didn't say anything else about hunting me or Les Jerome down for revenge. At least, I wasn't told anything like that."

"Well, it would be good to find out what kind of life he's building for himself these days," Mal said. "It's possible I can learn if he is in fact living in Las Vegas, and even what he's doing. Law enforcement is good at networking. And my being a former Marine is even better...I know a detective in Vegas who I served with in the South Pacific."

Augusta had to smile. "You do have old Marine buddies all over the country, don't you? One in Vegas, one in Texas, another up the road in Dayton...."

The tension broken, the group relaxed. "Get a good night's sleep," Mal said to Allan. "I'll contact my friend tomorrow. Since you're out on bond, your movements aren't restricted. Gus tells me there's a rehearsal for *Hoffmann* tomorrow and you're free to attend."

"You should be there," Augusta said. "We're doing the staging for Act One—the 'Olympia' Act. And after we're finished, I can give you the movement for the Prologue, and then you're caught up."

"I don't know." Allan ran his hand over the back of his head. "I'd really like to come, it would sure take my mind off being an accused murderer. But what about the rest of the cast? How will they feel about me being there? I'd think my arrest will be in the news tomorrow."

"Most of the people in the cast know you and will know as surely as we do that there's no way you killed anybody. That cast will become your team, I can guarantee that." Augusta stood.

"We all need a good night's sleep. This is a nightmare, Allan, but I'm sure it will quickly be resolved. I'll pick you up tomorrow before rehearsal."

She hugged him warmly, Dennis and Mal each shook his hand, and the three of them left the house. Augusta shivered slightly in the cold air and Mal pulled her close.

They stood with Dennis beside his car as Mal asked, "What about the people at his VFW post? I know you spend time there and have a good idea how people interact."

"Allan is a great favorite. He does everything he can for anyone who needs any help with anything. I've never seen any indication of Allan having problems with any of the vets there. It's been a big help to him to reach out to them. I've seen quite a change in recent months."

Dennis turned to Augusta. "I pray you're right about this being resolved quickly. Allan doesn't need this hanging over him."

"Pray for more than that," Mal said. "Pray we find the real killer, and the proof we need to arrest that person."

They said their goodnights, and once headed toward home, Malcolm remarked, "Leslie Jerome needs to be investigated as well. The Sheriff's Office won't do that; they think they have the perpetrator. Did he have enemies? Could one of them be the person who shot him and planted the gun in Allan's car? It would have to have been someone who knew them both."

"Which brings us right back to Luke Bridges." Augusta turned toward Malcolm. "One way for Luke to get revenge on both of them and get off scot free. He shoots Leslie, plants the gun in Allan's car."

"Yes, I had the same thought. And we need to deal with the motive according to the sheriff: both men were interested in the same woman. Someone needs to talk to Marissa tomorrow. And maybe the nosy neighbor has more to say." His jaw tightened. "Damn, I wish the CPD had this case. I can't send Danny or Jim to investigate, so Garrett or someone in his office will need to do that."

Augusta sighed. "If you learn Luke is not living in Las Vegas…you're thinking it's possible he's right here? Living somewhere in Hamilton County, maybe even in Cincinnati?"

"Well, if he is, I'm sure he's not calling himself Luke Bridges. Remember his background, Augusta. I think that bunch gets a class in 'Assumed Identities 101' when they're kids. It's a waste of time to check residency lists. And he certainly knows how to stay out of sight, as well as how to get out of town faster than a speeding bullet."

Augusta shivered. "I know I told you about Allan having a strange feeling a few times that someone was watching him. Maybe even stalking him?"

"Frank Barker is living in Vegas, but he's with the Clark County Sheriff's Office. Law enforcement out there has been overwhelmed with this influx of members of organized crime that have taken over that whole area recently."

Mal checked his watch. "It's nearly eleven, so it's about eight in Vegas. I'll call the Sheriff's Office when we get home. It's unlikely Frank Barker would be there this late on a Saturday, but you never know. He might get my message and call back tomorrow." He took a closer look at his wife. "Lots of bad memories, I'm sure. Those days Nunzio Ponti had you in captivity were the worst of my life, and I'm sure yours."

"I wondered if we'd ever see each other again," she whispered.

Mal put an arm around her and Augusta unbuckled her seat belt and moved as close to him as she could, resting her head on his shoulder.

"Mal, are we ever going to have the Ponti family completely out of our lives?"

Susan Moore Jordan

Chapter Eight
Multiple Personalities

Sunday, March 8
1:15 p.m.

"After Dennis and I both talked to her, Mom decided to stay in Baltimore for the present."

Allan clutched his *Hoffmann* score on the drive to Music Hall, as if it gave him some strength or possibly solace. "She was glad to know I'm not locked up and have rehearsals to attend. I doubt we convinced her there was nothing to worry about, though." A sigh. "Hell, I'm plenty worried myself. Right now I still don't know if it's a good idea for me to be at this rehearsal."

"We need you here. You need to be here." Augusta pulled into a parking spot near Music Hall. "Just concentrate on what you need to do to create this complex character. Your musical preparation has been exceptional. You can sing Hoffmann's nemesis in your sleep. Now you need to figure him out."

Strains of piano music from the stage in the main auditorium alerted them to Thomas Schippers' having arrived earlier. "Listen to that. He's an amazing pianist. He's a superb conductor. Is there anything the man can't do?" Augusta was in awe of Maestro Schippers.

Allan's mood improved instantly. "Working with him is a dream. Working with the two of you is…heaven."

"What a compliment."

Three of the Conservatory students were waiting to enter the auditorium and made a point of speaking with Allan, shaking his hand and then embracing him.

"Are we ever glad you're here!" "Great to see you. You know we're a hundred percent behind you, right?" "Onward and upward, my man."

Allan smiled warmly and it seemed to Augusta he visibly relaxed. In his element with colleagues, working together to create their vision of Offenbach's masterpiece.

Wonder what exactly Dennis and Allan said to Maureen Meissner? And I wonder how I'd react if something like this happened to Ryan or Danny? Would I be able to trust that their friends could right a wrong? She decided it probably was better for Maureen to wait until more came to light. After all, Allan's arraignment, scheduled for the next morning, might provide more information about what Lieutenant Vogel's detectives had unearthed.

She also knew Maureen handled herself remarkably well in any situation, a strength her son had inherited. Maureen, five years a widow, served as branch manager for a large bank in Baltimore, an impressive achievement for a woman. She also had family in that city to give her support—two brothers and a sister, plus numerous nieces and nephews. Even more, she would have thoroughly discussed with Allan what he would prefer her to do and accepted his wishes over her own inclination. Augusta also knew she had travel plans to attend the performances, just twelve days away, with some of those family members. Augusta's fervent wish continued to be that this would be resolved within a few days. Maybe even on Monday, with any luck.

Determined to focus on the opera, she asked the cast to find seats while she gave them staging notes for the first act. It pleased her to see the cast making Allan feel they needed him there, just as she had known they would.

Once again, George van Dorn was filling in for Hoffmann. For this act, George was able to work from memory since the "Olympia" act had been part of an opera workshop presentation not long ago, and he had performed the role of Hoffmann. Allan had also been part of that production as Dr. Coppelius, but the emphasis had been on fantasy rather than the dual personalities of his character.

Irene Madison was on hand in the role of Nicklausse, and a rising coloratura presently performing with an opera company in Germany, Sylvia Cabrini, would join them for the final dress rehearsals the following week. Since Olympia is a mechanical doll—a role Cabrini performed frequently—much of her staging was the same used by many opera companies, and

Augusta had written the performer and spoken with her on the phone in order to incorporate that staging into the Cincinnati performances. Such arrangements were not unusual in "Opera World" and the rest of the cast imagined their Olympia as Schippers played and sometimes sang her lines.

Allan's character in this act, Dr. Coppelius, along with his partner, Spalanzani, had invented a lovely life-sized doll. Coppelius provided Hoffmann with a pair of magic glasses which made Olympia appear to him as a real woman. Hoffmann fell in love with her, despite a warning from Nicklausse. When Spalanzani introduced Olympia at a party, she sang one of the best-known coloratura arias in opera.

The entire cast joined her in some sections of her aria, and there was much laughter on the stage. Augusta joined in and even Allan, offstage for the party scene, laughed heartily. This act was the most fun of the opera, though it ended with Allan's character, Dr. Coppelius, in a fit of rage destroying his own creation by tearing her to pieces when he learned the check he had received for her was worthless.

Augusta stopped the rehearsal. "At this point, we're glad to have our genius set designer, Larry Rogers, working magic for us so we don't have to actually dismember Olympia." The cast howled with laughter. "As this scene is often staged, after Olympia begins to dance out of control, she'll exit stage left, followed by Spalanzani. And as you probably already know, you'll be horrified to see pieces of her being thrown from the wings onto the stage." Smiles all around. "You can act horrified, right?" More laughter.

"Five pieces…two arms, two legs, torso. Then Dr. Coppelius enters from the wings carrying her head and Hoffmann finally realizes who…or rather, what…he's fallen in love with."

"And then I drag him offstage," Irene/Nicklausse volunteered

"You certainly do," Augusta agreed.

Irene spit on one hand and then the other, gleefully rubbing her hands together. "I can do that."

More laughter from the cast.

Throughout the rehearsal, it was apparent Allan immersed himself into the role and there was no thought about him being a murder suspect. Maestro Schippers, highly pleased, praised the cast for a first-rate rehearsal and told them he was happy he'd been able to play for them. More hugs for Allan as the singers left. Augusta gathered up her materials and the two of them headed back to her car.

Allan, in good spirits on the drive back to Milly's house, became thoughtful. "I've been thinking about my role in this opera. Four characters…am I right in thinking it's one character who has four distinct personalities? Is that even possible? I've heard of 'split personalities,' but aren't they just dual personalities? You know, like Dr. Jekyll and Mr. Hyde?"

"I think there have been cases of multiple personalities. It's a severe psychotic break, I would surmise."

Allan sat silently for a few moments. "Two things that intrigue me. First, what kind of event or events could cause the psychotic break that splits one personality into several? Second, I wonder if a person that's happened to would even be aware of what was going on? I would guess not. He thinks he's still only himself, completely unaware of the damage caused by his...alter personality...or personalities."

Silence again, then Allan continued. "This character, Dr. Coppelius. Right away we see his distrust of people. That becomes rage at the end of the act. In the Prologue, Lindorf is haughty and arrogant. So between the Prologue and the Olympia act we meet two of the personalities of Hoffmann's nemesis. With each iteration he becomes more prone to violence of some kind." He thought for a moment. "Violence can be psychological as well as physical, in my opinion."

"Definitely. I think with the nemesis character, it sometimes can be both," Augusta remarked.

"In the Giulietta act, Dapertutto is manipulative and deceitful. In the final act, Dr. Miracle is controlling and bent on causing Antonia's death. He doesn't strangle her, but I think he's capable of that."

Then, abruptly: "You know, I really have to wonder if it could be Luke Bridges who's trying to pin Leslie Jerome's murder on me. And he killed Les. I can't think of anyone else I've ever known who would do something so...vicious. I'm still processing all of this."

"Yes, of course you are. Malcolm should know by tomorrow about Luke's whereabouts, and I have a strong feeling he's not going to be in Las Vegas."

"Which would mean he could be here in Ohio. The more I think about it, the more it seems a real possibility. You know, if he is here, I'm sure he's not using his real name. Just like Bobby when he went into witness protection, Luke would have to hide who he really is. Maybe he's using the Italian version of his name, Luca Ponti."

"Probably not. I think the name Ponti would raise a red flag here in Cincinnati."

They rode silently for a time, and then Allan said slowly, "Augusta, I wonder if you shouldn't replace me in this production. We don't know what's going to happen."

"Absolutely not." This didn't surprise her; she'd thought of it as well. Suppose their best efforts failed and they couldn't find the real killer before the show went up? What would that do to ticket sales, to audience reaction? Even more of a concern, what would it do to Allan? If there was a trial it would be months in the future and everything would be in limbo. Augusta found that unacceptable.

"The killer will be found quickly. I'm convinced of that. And you'll be cleared and create an incredible character in this production. And do extremely well at the Met competition later this month."

Allan allowed himself a small smile. "As Golde would say, from your lips to God's ears."

"*Fiddler on the Roof.* There's another great role for you, Allan. Tevye."

"That's musical theater," Allan said.

"*Great* musical theater. Who says you can't do both…opera and musical theater?"

Allan grinned more broadly. "Wouldn't that be another kind of 'split personality?'"

Augusta laughed. "I guess you could look at it that way. It's been done before. Don't forget *South Pacific* and Ezio Pinza. Another great basso."

"And he even won a Tony," Allan added. "Well, as I said…from your lips to God's ears, Augusta."

Chapter Nine
One Man in His Time Plays Many Parts

Monday, March 9

Augusta canceled her Monday lessons so she could accompany Allan to his arraignment that morning. She had decided she wanted to be free for the afternoon in case there might be some way she could help Garrett. Nothing had yet surfaced about another viable suspect for Leslie Jerome's murder and at the arraignment Allan would be charged, plead not guilty, confirm to the judge that Garrett Stoddard was his attorney and be given a date for his preliminary hearing.

Allan was extremely nervous at the courthouse. The man who had been a confident artist at the rehearsal on Sunday seemed rattled by the fact this case was moving forward again. Garrett gave him a pep talk before they left for court, but Allan's concern was also because he would have to tell his mother he'd be in court again for a preliminary hearing later in the week.

Augusta did her best to reassure him, but she thought if it had been her in this position, she'd no doubt feel the same way he did. The murder weapon was a strong piece of evidence.

The arraignment took only moments, and the preliminary hearing was set for Thursday morning at ten. The three of them returned to Garrett's car.

"Look, Mal is probably talking to his friend in Las Vegas right now and getting some information about Luke Bridges," Garrett said. "I need to interview Marissa Keyes and also the woman in Jerome's apartment building who has become Detective Herb Vogel's best friend. How reliable a witness is she, anyway? What kind of a person spends her time spying on her neighbors?"

Allan, seated next to Garrett, stared out of the window. Augusta wanted to hug him and tell him it was going to be all right, but she didn't really know that. As of now they were still at square one.

"Garrett, may I go with you to talk to Marissa Keyes?" she asked. "Maybe as your unofficial assistant? I'm pretty intuitive. Women sometimes open up more in the presence of a sympathetic female."

"Might not be a bad idea," Garrett said. "I know all about your intuition."

"Mom's expecting me to call her," Allan said. "What am I going to say? 'Nothing much happened, but don't worry. It's going to be fine. I don't know how, but it's going to be fine.'"

"Tell her you're hard at work on the opera, you know that people who care about you are doing everything they can to find the person who did this, and for the moment that's where we are," Augusta soothed.

She leaned forward and rested a hand on his shoulder. "Tell her the opera production is going to be great and it's an honor to be working with Thomas Schippers. Tell her things happen when they're supposed to happen and you have faith you'll be on stage on March twentieth, having been exonerated." She squeezed the shoulder. "And I believe every word I just said."

They pulled up at Milly's house. "I'm trusting you to work on your music as Augusta suggested," Garrett said to Allan. "We won't be gone long. If the phone rings, don't answer it. It might be reporters trying to track you down. After Augusta and I talk to Miss Keyes, we'll come back here. Hopefully by then Malcolm will have some information for us."

***

Marissa Keyes, a trim, attractive woman with long blonde hair, did her best to appear pleased to see them. However, her eyes, red from crying and lack of sleep, made obvious her heartbreak at losing Leslie and her worry about Allan. She offered them coffee which they accepted, and they sat together at her dining table.

"The sheriff's detectives interviewed me," Marissa began. "First they asked me about my…alibi for that night. I told them I had dinner with two girlfriends from work and we went to a movie, a Burt Lancaster thriller called 'Airport.' Then they asked me about my relationship with Leslie and Allan, how we all met—it seemed like they thought it could be have been some kind of scandalous love triangle."

"Looking for motive," Augusta murmured to Garrett.

Marissa continued, "Which of course it wasn't. I met Allan first, soon after he moved in, and invited him for coffee not long after that. I knew he was a singer and a voice teacher, and I love opera. I'd seen him perform at the Conservatory and especially appreciated his great Mephistopheles in *Faust*. It was lovely to meet him and discuss opera. I don't have many friends who are as enthusiastic as I am, and certainly no family members, sad to say." She smiled wistfully. "Then when he introduced me to his friend Leslie, our shared love of opera and appreciation for Allan's talent was an instant connection."

"But it became something more," Augusta suggested.

"Yes, it did. Very quickly." Her eyes flashed. "You know…the detectives who interviewed me tried hard to insinuate that Allan and I must have been lovers. We never were, there was no intimacy. We were…we *are* great friends, something people need. It surprised me that the CPD isn't handling this case. I think I might have had a much different experience."

"The crime took place in Elmwood Place, which is a village nearly surrounded by Cincinnati, but with their own police department. Because their department is small, the mayor requested the Hamilton County Sheriff's Office to take over the case," Garrett explained. "Herb Vogel's detectives are quite capable, though I'm sorry to hear you had an unfortunate experience with them."

Marissa pressed her lips together. "Perhaps I misjudged them. In any event, I hope they left here convinced Allan and I were never lovers, we were friends. For one thing, I'm thirty-four. Allan is twenty-nine."

Garrett lifted an eyebrow at Augusta. "Your relationship with Leslie Jerome was quite different, then."

"You know, my husband is younger than I am," Augusta interjected. "The age difference was something I struggled with when we first became involved. And I believe it's common knowledge that he moved in with me before we celebrated our marriage."

Marissa looked at Augusta for a moment, digesting this information, "Yes, Allan is younger than I am, but really, in our case age had nothing to do with it. You know…either the spark is there or it isn't." She gazed thoughtfully at Augusta. "I'm sure you have many men friends, some close, some not, right?"

"I do indeed. One is a priest, as a matter of fact. One of the most attractive men I've ever met. We're very close friends and fellow teachers at Cliffside College. But there has never been anything the least bit romantic about our friendship. No 'spark.'"

Augusta leaned forward and continued, "This is very personal, but may I ask when you and Leslie became close?"

Marissa seemed eager to respond. "Well, as I said, there was definitely a spark there from the first time we met. We began to see each other regularly, and fairly often we would invite Allan to join us for dinner. The weekend Allan performed for the Regional Met Auditions Les and I took him to Indiana University so he wouldn't have to drive."

She smiled at the memory. "He stayed in the men's dorm. Les and I took a room at a motel." A pause. "That was the weekend we became lovers."

Marissa stood and moved to a window. "And the first time we talked about marriage." She stared outside, struggling to keep the tears at bay. "We were just beginning to make some definite decisions the last time I saw him."

"And you never saw signs that Allan was jealous or angry about your relationship with Captain Jerome?" Garrett asked.

"Good heavens, no. Allan seemed happy for us. We were all good friends. I remember one night at dinner he joked about hanging out his shingle as a matchmaker after his success with Les and me." This memory brought tears to her eyes, and she fumbled for a handkerchief in her pocket.

"Allan is a great guy. He's unusually tall, and maybe that can seem menacing to some…but he's kind and gentle. Could he have killed Les? Not in a million years."

Garrett had what he needed. "Thank you so much for speaking with us, Marissa. I know this is stressful, and you've been a great help. If it becomes necessary…and I sincerely hope it will not…you'll be a strong witness for Allan."

Once back in the car, Garrett commented, "Thanks for coming with me. I'm not sure she would have told me some of that if you hadn't been there. I meant what I said, she's *our* witness. If we have a trial, the prosecutor might even find it necessary to treat her as a hostile witness."

"You said *if* we have a trial."

"As I told Marissa, I sincerely hope it will not come to that. Let's swing by Mal's office and see what he can tell us about Luke Bridges' whereabouts."

***

"I was able to confirm there is a Luke Bridges, a Vietnam vet, in the crime family in Las Vegas. Presently, Luke is in the wind," Malcolm said as the three of them sat together in his office in City Hall. "My friend in Vegas tells me he has a few undercovers keeping tabs on the whole Ponti gang. Luke Bridges left Las Vegas at least four months ago, maybe longer. They'll do some digging to see if they can find out more."

"Your Marine friend is in charge of undercover cops?" Augusta's eyes widened. "That must be fascinating. And challenging, I would think. Especially in a city such as Las Vegas."

"Yes, I really lucked out when I talked to him. The Pontis generally try to keep a low profile, but that's not easy for them."

"Well, my experience with Bobby Bridges would certainly confirm that," Augusta commented. "Of course, when he started having problems at the

91

Conservatory, I had no idea he was a member of a crime family."

"Sorry to say, you've learned more about this particular crime family than you ever wanted to know," Mal said.

He turned to Garrett. "One more thing—they're faxing me a photo of Luke. If you want to wait a bit, you can take it to Allan to confirm if it's the same Luke Bridges he knew in Vietnam. I'm betting it is. How did things go this morning?"

"Routine. Stressful for Allan," Augusta replied. "He's supposed to be working on music, we have another rehearsal Wednesday evening. Hopefully that will keep him occupied."

"You okay with hanging around a little longer to get the picture?" Garrett asked Augusta.

"Sure. I'm always fine hanging out with Captain Mitchell." She batted her eyelashes at her husband, who laughed.

"Want me to give you two some privacy?" Garrett quipped. "I see the spark is still there."

"Do you mind telling me what Garrett's talking about?" Mal asked Augusta.

"Marissa Keyes. She said when she first met Leslie Jerome, there was a definite spark between them." Augusta sighed. "It's so sad, Mal. They had just started seriously considering marriage. I know Allan is very concerned about Marissa. I'm sure the detectives took his concern completely the wrong way when they talked to him."

"Possibly, but talking to Marissa was heartening. It appears she tried to set them straight in no uncertain terms," Garrett said.

Jim Edmonds, Mal's former partner who now partnered with his son Dan, tapped on the door and stuck his head in. "The photo just came in. Want to take a look at it?"

"Thanks, Jim. Can you make a copy for Garrett first?"

"Roger that, Chief. It'll only take a minute."

Mal turned again to his wife. "How do you think Allan is doing?"

"I think the absolute best thing for him right now is focus on *The Tales of Hoffmann*. Being at rehearsal yesterday was a great help to him."

"I remember him as Dr. Miracle in that workshop production a few years ago," Mal said. "Allan was great in the role, even then. Maybe it's partly because of his height, but he can be imposing and intimidating."

"Well, Dr. Miracle is the last of four characters he plays. Or rather, the four personalities of one character— Hoffman's nemesis. He manages to destroy Hoffmann's attempts at finding a woman to love. Each of the personalities he portrays becomes more vicious than the previous one. It's one of the greatest basso roles in opera."

"Here's hoping," Garrett said, "that being imposing and intimidating doesn't work against him in this real life situation."

Chapter Ten
Memories and Music

Augusta and Garrett found Allan in better spirits. Reviewing the music of the "Giulietta" act of Offenbach's opera apparently had been helpful.

With keen interest, Allan studied the photo Garrett handed him. "Yes, this is definitely the guy I knew in Vietnam. What did Mal find out about him?"

"He hasn't been in Las Vegas for the past few months, but…." Augusta turned to Garrett, wondering how much she should say about the Clark County Sheriff's department having undercover cops watching the Ponti/Bridges family.

"There may be a way the police there can find out more about Luke's whereabouts," Garrett finished. Augusta glanced at him gratefully.

"You can be sure Malcolm will be all over this," she said to Allan.

"It's incredible that you guys made the connection with the Newport Bridges. And definitely upsetting to think that Luke could be the one behind this," Allan said.

"We all want to help you," Augusta said with a smile. "Well, if you're doing okay, I'm going to take my car and head home."

"I'm fine. I talked to my mother, and she is as well. Milly offered to play through the 'Giulietta' act for me tomorrow so I'll be well prepared for Wednesday's rehearsal."

Driving home, Augusta thought about the photo of Luke Bridges she had seen: an attractive soldier in uniform. Straight dark hair, military crew cut, no smile. Piercing eyes. Clean-shaven, of course. *I see a resemblance to Bobby.* Memories of Nunzio Ponti holding her captive in the basement of a home in her own neighborhood threatened to surface and she pushed them away.

For distraction, Augusta flipped on the car radio. As she started to turn the dial to the classical music station, she heard the announcement, "Here's the top tune on the charts today, Simon and Garfunkel's 'Bridge Over Troubled Water.'"

'Bridge,' indeed, she thought, *how appropriate. Allan is right, linking Luke to the Newport Bridges was a huge break. Now all we have to do is find him...and tie him to this case.*

She wondered if Bobby Bridges had managed to stay in witness protection. He had left once and come back to Cincinnati to try to see Danny's wife Martha, and could have been killed by family members seeking revenge against him for helping save Augusta. The U.S. Marshal's office had returned him to the program and sent him to a new location. Mal had been surprised; he said that seldom happened. People in the witness protection program were free to leave but once they did, they were on their own.

I wonder if Martha has heard from him since then. That was what...five years ago? At least. Chances are she hasn't. On the other hand....

***

Tuesday, March 10

Tuesday mornings were one of Augusta's days at Cliffside College, where she taught a class in Music Appreciation as well as teaching voice students. She spoke with Milly early in the day and was assured Allan seemed fine, spending time on the *Hoffmann* music as well as his arias for the Met audition. Claudia Prince had agreed to cover teaching his voice students until after the hearing on Thursday, at which time everyone fervently hoped he would no longer be under suspicion of having killed Leslie Jerome.

Let's hope Malcolm learns more from his friend in Las Vegas today, and is able to track down Luke Bridges...or whatever he might be calling himself at present.

Augusta decided to stop by Danny and Martha's house on her way home from Cliffside. Her car radio was tuned to WGUC, Cincinnati's classical music station, and she found it highly satisfactory to hear the last movement of Rachmaninoff's Third Piano Concerto, one of her favorites. She heard it as a triumphant declaration of music filling the universe as nothing else could. It always made her aware of how fortunate she was to be enjoying a life in music.

Martha certainly had managed to do that as well. She continued to sing professionally, mainly in the tri-state area—Ohio, Kentucky, Indiana. She would perform two good roles in the coming Summer Opera season, Micaëla in *Carmen* and Musetta in *La Boheme*. So far, she balanced being a wife and mother to a young child with pursuing a career quite capably, with help from her family in caring for Maxie when she was away.

Maxie answered the door, wrestling with it a little but finally opening it wide. Augusta bent down and swooped him up. At nearly three, he was an intriguing combination of baby and little boy. As always, Augusta was struck by his resemblance to Mal—in particular, the same dark blue eyes, though he had Martha's fair skin and blond hair.

Martha and Danny's home in Westwood sat in a comfortable neighborhood, an older house built in the twenties or thirties, two stories and a basement. Augusta appreciated Martha's choices in decorating her home; they were similar to hers. Soft blues and greens in the living room, wallpaper in the dining room in a simple floral design. Maxie's room was a delight and a true little boy's room; he had graduated to a youth bed recently. Bins for his numerous toys and a bookshelf. A rocking horse, toy piano, and miniature drum set were also part of the décor. Balloons of different colors decorated the light blue wallpaper.

"I'm glad to see you, Grammy. Come watch me play the piano." Maxie clutched her hand and pulled her with him. Martha stood by the piano, smiling, as Maxie climbed up onto the bench, sitting directly in the center. Augusta watched as he carefully positioned his hands on the keyboard and played a two-note chord with his left hand as he moved up and down a five-note scale with his right hand, three times.

He turned and gave Augusta a brilliant smile as she applauded and said, "Bravo! That's wonderful! When did you learn that?"

"We were just practicing it," Martha replied. "How nice that you stopped by today. Maxie has been asking if we could call you to invite you to see his recital." Max looked from one of them to the other and climbed off the bench. His mother and grandmother applauded, and Maxie joined in, clapping vigorously.

"Can I have my cookies now?" He asked his mother.

"Of course. They're ready on the kitchen table. Let me talk to Grammy for a minute and we'll come and join you."

Maxie ran happily into the kitchen and Martha continued, "I'm glad to see you. Of course, I am concerned about Allan. We had such a great rehearsal last week with Maestro Schippers, and I've been looking forward to staging the act Saturday. Is that still going to happen?"

"I'm planning on it. The 'Giulietta' act tomorrow night, then our Saturday morning rehearsal for 'Antonia.' Dress rehearsals next Monday and Wednesday nights."

"Let's sit down for a minute, shall we?" Martha invited. "What's going on with the case? Danny tells me they've learned this guy…Luke Bridges…isn't in Las Vegas, but that's about all he's said. And probably all he should tell me."

"So you know Luke Bridges is a member of the Ponti family." Augusta smiled as she heard Maxie singing in the kitchen. "Listen to that. He's trying to sing your aria."

"There is certainly music in that little soul," Martha agreed. "He's definitely my child. Even Danny admits that."

"You know, ever since we found out about Luke Bridges I've had Bobby on my mind. He's supposed to be in the witness protection program…but I wondered, have you heard from him?" Augusta watched Martha closely as she spoke, and saw a slight flush.

"Why would I hear from him?"

A dead giveaway, Augusta thought. *Answering a question with another question.*

"I thought so. I'm guessing since you've been married to Dan, Bobby probably sends letters to your family's address and they pass them on to you. Is he still where he's supposed to be?"

Martha sighed. "Yes, I've had a few letters from him over the years, but there's no return address so I couldn't reply…not that I wanted to."

She paused for a moment. "You know, that's not completely true, Augusta. The last time he wrote, he sent me a return address and a phone number and asked me to get in touch with him. He's left WITSEC again and is living in northern California, under another name. I haven't told Danny about this last letter and I must do that, but of course I never intend to contact Bobby again."

"When did you receive that letter?"

"Just last week."

"Do you still have it?"

Martha shook her head. "No, I don't keep them. I tell Danny about them and throw them away. I probably shouldn't even have read them…but I guess I was curious. I couldn't believe what Bobby did when he first left the witness protection program and took a bus back to Cincinnati. I don't know what he expected from me when he showed up here."

"He expected you to tell him you were madly in love with him, you know that. He wanted you to reciprocate the feelings he had for you. And it's obvious he still does."

Martha glanced toward the kitchen, but Maxie apparently was happily occupied with cookies and milk. "I never gave him any reason to think I was interested in him. I was nice because I felt sorry for him. But I always told him he needed to find somebody else."

"That last letter…what else did he say about being in California and using another name?"

"He's working with a voice teacher and hopes to do some auditions. He changed his name to something Italian…Benedetto something. Not Ponti, though. But something similar. Maybe Conti? He said he's living near San Francisco."

"Since he's lost his protection, he must realize he may be in some danger."

"He said he just wants to sing again. I can understand that, and I'm more grateful than I can say about being able to continue to perform. My parents have been wonderful about taking care of Maxie when I need to be away. Danny has, too. So far it's worked out well."

"Mommy!" from the kitchen.

Augusta stood. "Let's go enjoy my grandson. But Martha, please let me know if you hear from Bobby again. Since he's been away from his family for several years I doubt he'd know anything about Luke. On the other hand, he may be in touch with his family."

Martha fluffed the pillows on the couch. "That's entirely possible. They were very close. And of course I'll keep you posted."

The two women moved toward the kitchen as Martha added, "You may have to listen to your grandson play drums. Can you deal with that?"

"Of course I can," Augusta laughed. "I'm not too sure I could live with it every day, though."

Chapter Eleven
Life Imitating Art?

"The guy we think may be in Luke Bridges' crosshairs confirmed that the photo is the same man he served with in Vietnam." Malcolm, elbows resting on his desk, phone tucked under his chin, peered closely at the photo.

Lieutenant Frank Barker, now heading up the Vice Squad for the Clark County Sheriff's Department, had been one of the Marines closest to Malcolm during their time in the South Pacific. More than once they'd had each other's backs, and Mal believed Frank had saved his life during one battle.

"Well, my guys tell me they've been asking around, and they confirm no one has seen Luke here in Vegas for maybe the past four months, and no one knows where he went. You think he may be the one who killed the Vietnam vet and is after another he blames for his problems over there, right? So he may have decided to even the score and could be in Cincinnati."

"It seems like a strong possibility," Mal replied. "Allan Meissner told my wife he's had an uneasy feeling about being watched, or maybe even stalked."

"I'm sure if Luke was doing that, he wouldn't want Meissner to recognize him. Our people doing undercover know all kinds of tricks to make themselves look different, as you know."

Mal studied the photo. "Let his hair grow out for starters. Long sideburns, long on the top. Maybe those ducktails. Kind of a combination Elvis and Beatles look."

"Long sideburns, long on top…sometimes down to the eyebrows," Frank confirmed.

"Wonder how I'd look in one of those," Mal mused, and Frank chuckled.

"Not like a 'top cop,' that's for sure. Luke's hair looks dark in the picture. Maybe he'd dye it so he could find out if it's true 'blonds have more fun.'"

Mal laughed. "Well, that would be a start. Maybe put on some pounds? He looks pretty trim in this photo."

"How about growing some facial hair? That would certainly change his appearance," Frank suggested.

"A full beard would be too obvious, I think. But a moustache might make sense." Mal tried to visualize those changes as he again gazed at the photo.

"You know…a different hair style, a moustache, and big dark glasses and this guy could very well be unrecognizable," Frank said.

"Yeah, that could do the trick," Mal agreed. "I'll have the photo doctored in several different combinations and show them to Allan. He might be able to identify his stalker. He's a pretty observant guy."

They exchanged pleasantries and Mal hung up his phone. A tap on his door, and Augusta opened it.

"I know this isn't correct protocol, but Jim said he didn't see a problem with me letting you know I'm here."

Mal, happy to see her, stood and strode around his desk to give her a warm embrace.

"Oh, my, Chief Mitchell. I think I may drop in unannounced more often," she said, returning the embrace.

Mal still marveled that this remarkable woman was now his wife. When they first met, he had been drawn to her despite their confrontational meeting. He soon learned to appreciate her spirit and intelligence, and before long he even recalled having admired her years earlier on stage at the Summer Opera in the role of Frasquita in *Carmen*. Meeting her again reawakened the attraction he had felt. That she was seven years older was never a consideration for him, though he had to convince her it was not.

He pulled a chair up close to his desk for Augusta and returned to his seat. "To what do I owe the pleasure of this visit?"

"I thought I'd stop by and see how things are going. I just spent a few minutes with our wonderful grandson, who played the piano for me."

Mal lifted an eyebrow and Augusta added, "No, really. Perfect posture, perfect hand position...those tiny hands...he played a two-note chord with his left hand,

and a five-note scale with his right hand. Mal, he's not quite three years old. That's pretty darned good."

"Yeah, he's something, all right. Nice that you could spend a little time with him."

She gazed into his eyes. "But I came to see how you are. It must be incredibly frustrating for you to not be involved in this murder investigation…and looking for puzzle pieces."

"You've got that right. I have to be careful since Dan Tehan's people are in charge." He sighed.

"Do you know if they've learned of any enemies Leslie Jerome might have had?"

"Why would they look? They're sure they've got their killer. The gun is pretty damning evidence. Allan's been arrested and charged. But I don't think they've found anything else. I know they searched Allan's apartment. There was nothing to find. I don't have anything against the detectives in the sheriff's office, but I don't think they can approach the skills of the men under my command."

Augusta leaned forward. "Have they talked to Marissa Keyes again? When Garrett and I talked to her, she said she felt the detectives from the Sheriff's Office mainly wanted her to confirm that there was a love triangle involved—which she vehemently denied."

Mal rested his elbows on his desk, clasping his hands together. "If I could talk to her the first thing I would ask about would be if there were any possible enemies Leslie might have mentioned. I think I need to ask Garrett to re-interview her."

"I could do that for you," Augusta said. "You know I just love to talk to people who might have information about a crime you're investigating." She batted her eyelashes, and Mal had to laugh.

"Yes, you do. And sitting here staring at the walls when I'm itching to learn more is about to make me stir crazy. I think I understand better why you sometimes insert yourself when you shouldn't."

Augusta picked up the picture from Malcolm's desk. "Are you memorizing this?"

"I was just on the phone with Frank Barker. Speculating about how Bridges might change his appearance if he's in town and doesn't want Allan to recognize him." He shared with her what he and Frank had discussed.

"Yes, I can see how that would definitely make him look different." She studied the photo. "Hair over his forehead, a moustache, long sideburns…add the dark glasses and he'd certainly be difficult to recognize." She handed him the photo.

Mal leaned back in his chair. "Speaking of the Bridges family, here's an interesting piece of information. We contacted the U.S. Marshal's Office. Bobby Bridges walked away from WITSEC again, and this time, they washed their hands of him. He split about a year and a half ago, and nobody at the agency knows…or cares…where he is."

Augusta glanced past Malcolm. "Oh…that is interesting. And really, not surprising. Bobby never knew when to leave well enough alone."

"How is Allan today?"

"He's hanging in there. Anxious, but trying hard to focus on the opera. And on the competition for the Metropolitan Opera at the end of the month. Those two events coming so close together concerned me, but maybe it's excellent that he has to keep his focus there."

"You know, bride…there's one person in the 'crime family members we have known' list that we haven't talked about." Mal leaned back and clasped his hands behind his head. "A man who thought he successfully left the Pontis. Changed his name and moved across the country, trying to get out of that family."

"Justin Manderley," she said. "You're right. And if he'd stayed in California, or Canada, he'd have been successful. But he made the mistake of coming to Cincinnati to visit the Parkside Playhouse and had the misfortune of witnessing a gangland-style killing just as he arrived there. And the Ponti goon recognized him. Justin…real name, Lorenzo Ponti…should have changed his appearance as well as his name. Too bad he didn't think about that."

Augusta continued, enjoying this memory. "That was quite an adventure for him…Justin, I mean. While he was hiding out in the Conservatory, we wondered if we had a ghost."

"All the while you were preparing a 'ghostly' opera workshop production," Malcolm recalled. He lifted his wife's left hand and kissed her fingers. "You did some great stuff to solve that one, Gus, and you ended up with this ring."

She leaned forward, pressing her palm to his cheek. "I wasn't so sure you thought what I did was great at the

time, Mal. You surprised me with the engagement ring."
A brief but tender kiss.

"Do you keep track of your ghost?" He grinned.

"He's mainly working in Canada, sometimes in California. I think he's being considered to direct a film, in fact. I'm sure he wants to continue keeping his distance from the Ponti family."

Augusta sighed. "Yet, here we are once again, trying to find yet another Ponti. Or Bridges." She gripped his arm, hard. "Mal, you have to find Luke Bridges. And soon. I have a bad feeling he may be planning to kill Allan if he starts to think his scheme to frame him for Leslie's murder is falling apart."

Mal picked up the photo. "I'll have this altered to show Allan and see where that gets us. You have another rehearsal tomorrow, if I remember correctly."

"Yes, at Music Hall at seven. What are you thinking?"

"I'm thinking it might be a good idea for Jim Edmonds to keep a protective eye on Allan. And he could get some culture and learn something about *The Tales of Hoffmann*."

Chapter Twelve
Oh, What a Tangled Web
We Weave…

Wednesday, March 11
1:00 a.m.

Augusta had far too much on her mind to get a good night's sleep, worrying about Allan and about her *Tales of Hoffmann* production. What if they couldn't get this cleared up quickly? The last thing she wanted to do was replace Allan in the opera. *Finding a replacement at this point would be next to impossible—our first performance is ten days away. And Allan needs this performance. He's going to be great in the role. What a business to have this happen now,* she thought with a sigh.

She stared at the ceiling, hearing strains of Offenbach's music in her head as she considered the case. *Malcolm and his friend in Las Vegas think the killer might be Luke Bridges. They're sure he's somehow changed his appearance, which means Allan may very well have been under surveillance those times he felt uneasy. No doubt if Luke is here in the Cincinnati area he's using another name, but how can we find out what that might be? Greater Cincinnati has a population of over a million people. Mal may have come up with an idea of how Luke might have changed his appearance, but how in the world can they find him quickly...or even at all...with that many people living here?* She continued to stare at the ceiling, looking for answers that weren't there..

Okay, some things in Allan's favor: no fingerprints at all on the gun. No gunpowder residue on his hands, Garrett told me they checked on that. But from what I've learned, it's unlikely it would still have been on his hands anyway; he wasn't arrested until hours after the shooting.

Augusta turned over gingerly, eyeing Malcolm, who remained in a deep sleep. *How is it that men can sleep so soundly, no matter what is going on? I wonder if Allan is sleeping?* Easing out of bed, she stepped into her slippers and quietly headed downstairs. Fritz, ever on alert, followed, and when she dropped into the comfortable sofa in the living room, he rested his chin on her knee as he whined softly.

Augusta stroked the silky head. *Another thing, there was no witness to the shooting. Nothing incriminating was found in Allan's apartment after a thorough search. And oh...this may be most important of all...Allan has lived an exemplary life. He's a decorated war veteran. He has two college degrees. He's a respected performer and teacher. All they have is the weapon, found in his car.*

Mal tells me it would have been easy for anyone to plant it. But at the moment, he's the only suspect the Sheriff's Office has for Leslie's murder. And they think they have a motive...but it's not corroborated.

Bobby Bridges came to mind again. *He may be out of WITSEC, but I'll bet he's been in touch with his family. I wonder if he even knew Luke? That bunch is pretty tight, my guess is that they may have known each other since childhood...they're about the same age. And Bobby might even know where Luke is. If only Martha hadn't thrown Bobby's last letter away.*

A sudden thought: *If Bobby was in or near San Francisco and itching to sing, it's certainly possible he may have auditioned for the San Francisco Opera. I wonder...could someone at the San Francisco Opera have heard from him about auditioning?*

Augusta went into the alcove with Fritz at her side. She stood by the window, gazing at her garden, dimly lit by a crescent moon. *It seems to me an employee of the— say, the Philadelphia Opera Company—might be interested in knowing more about Benedetto...what, Conti? Has he contacted them about a potential audition?*

Augusta reminded herself she'd recently promised Malcolm not to make any phone calls about a case without letting him know first. *But I won't be asking about the case. I'll just call to get Benedetto's contact information. Mainly, his phone number.*

Now that she had a plan of action, Augusta felt less frustrated about the current situation. She reached for a jar of dog treats they kept in the alcove and Fritz's tail wagged vigorously. She gave Fritz a treat, bent and hugged him. The two of them quietly tiptoed upstairs and returned to the bedroom. Augusta smiled as she glanced at Malcolm. He hadn't moved since she left. She slipped back into bed, careful not to wake him.

It might be better for Martha to call Bobby when I have his number. After all, he's been writing her occasionally this entire time. He's likely to hang up on anyone else, even me.

She began to turn names over in her head for the new Production Assistant for the Philadelphia Opera Company just before she fell asleep.

***

Because of the three-hour time difference, Augusta had to wait until lunchtime on Wednesday before calling the San Francisco Opera Company. She had decided "Sheryl Tiegen" was from Virginia, so she adopted a light Southern accent.

"Good mornin'! This is Sheryl Tiegen callin'. I'm the brand new Production Assistant for the opera company...I mean for the Philadelphia Opera Company. I'm lookin' for some information—can you help me?"

"Good afternoon, Sheryl. This is Judy Bonds, secretary to the director of the San Francisco Opera. How's the weather back East?"

Pleasant voice, Augusta noted. She was glad she'd had the good sense to check Philadelphia's weather before she called. "It still feels a little like winter, especially to me. Ah just moved up here from Virginia.

No snow, though." *Careful, Sheryl, don't overdo the accent.*

"I thought I heard a bit of a Southern accent," Judy said. "What can I help you with, Sheryl?"

"I've been searchin' all through the office for some papers and I'm afraid my predecessor may have misplaced them. Mr. Rudel—Mr. Julius Rudel—is interested in a young tenor who auditioned a while back…I think maybe last November…and he wanted to reach out to him about a possibility for next season. We can't find his contact information, unfortunately…and we wondered if he'd also contacted your company?"

"I'll see what I can do. Can you give me his name?"

"Oh, my, I guess I'd better do that." Sheryl giggled. "Sorry. Since we can't find his audition form, Mr. Rudel has been tryin' to remember. He's sure it was Italian, maybe Gustavo or Leonardo or Benedetto? Last name he thinks is Conti or somethin' like that."

"Hold on a minute and let me check." Judy was back quickly.

"This may be your tenor. He was here earlier in the fall, but he calls from time to time. Benedetto Conti. Mr. Rudel has a good memory."

"I'm sure that was him…thank you! Can you give me his phone number and address?"

Judy provided the necessary information. "Good luck, Sheryl. As I recall he has quite a fine voice. He wasn't interested in *comprimario* roles, though, you should be aware of that."

Sheryl giggled again. "I guess he don't…doesn't like playin' second fiddle, so to speak."

The women said their goodbyes and Augusta stared at the phone number. *Martha is definitely the person who needs to call Bobby. I can be right there and write notes to her. Malcolm couldn't possibly be angry about her making the contact. 'No harm, no foul,' as I've heard him say.*

***

It took a little doing, but Augusta persuaded Martha to help her play sleuth. "Once we learn whether or not Bobby knows if Luke is here in Cincinnati, we can take that to the CPD homicide detectives. They'll have to do this without stepping on the toes of the sheriff's detectives, but I would think they can do some investigating and keep it under wraps. It may be a wild goose chase, after all. Bobby may not know a thing."

"But you hope he does," Martha said, still skeptical.

"Absolutely. I want to get Allan out of this mess as quickly as possible."

"Well, I can't call him and start off by asking him if he knows a man named Luke Bridges. That will not be what he wants to hear."

Oh, good, she's in. "He wants to know you at least are concerned about him. I think it was a little upsetting for you to learn he's left the witness protection program and is living under an assumed name. He's playing a dangerous game."

"I am concerned. I always...felt a little sorry for Bobby. He was so *needy*."

116

"I know you have a speaker phone. If I'm right here listening, I can write notes and help you do this." She handed Martha a paper. "In fact, here are some thoughts I have about what you might ask him."

Martha read over the paper, nodding. "Yes, these will be good." She picked up the handset but replaced it abruptly. "Does Malcolm know we're doing this?"

"As I said, we may not find out anything at all. I didn't see any point in mentioning it unless we have something substantial. There's a good chance it won't be helpful. And in that case," she added quickly, "I'll tell him I suggested you call Bobby but nothing came of it."

Martha again lifted the handset. "Why do I have the feeling I may live to regret this?"

Susan Moore Jordan

Chapter Thirteen
...When First We Practice to Deceive

Martha's phone call to Bobby began well. She told him she'd been thinking about him and wanted to know more about what he was doing. He obviously was happy to hear from her as he talked about the operatic roles he'd learned, the good work he was doing with his teacher, and the auditions he'd attended and those he had coming up.

"I hear you're married," he told Martha. "But I also heard you're still singing. Tell me about that."

I wonder who he's heard from, Augusta thought. *Maybe a family member who's still living in Newport? A friend from his high school or college days?*

"Yes, and I also have a three-year-old son," Martha said. "But thanks to my family, I'm able to get away occasionally to accept some engagements." She raised her eyebrows at Augusta and mouthed, *How does he know all this?*

Their conversation continued and Augusta pointed to an item on the list she had given Martha. Martha explained to Bobby about singing in *The Tales of Hoffmann* at Music Hall, and added, "Do you remember Allan Meissner? He's in the cast as well. He's now on the voice faculty at the Conservatory. We were reminiscing recently about our time as students there, and your name came up."

"In a good way, I hope," Bobby laughed.

"Oh, yes. He reminded me what a terrific voice you have. Oh, and he met someone not long ago and wondered if he might be related to you. A guy named Luke Bridges."

"Yeah, he's my cousin. He was living in Las Vegas but he moved to Cincinnati about …oh, I think before Christmas. Where did Allan run into him?"

Martha rolled her eyes. "I'm…not sure. Is he working here?"

Silence on the other end of the line.

"You know something? I think this conversation is over, Martha. I've said too much."

An abrupt *click* and then a dial tone.

"Well, I think I just blew it," Martha said, replacing the handset.

"No, you did great. We know for sure now Luke is in Cincinnati," Augusta assured her. "Blabby Bobby, true to form, not thinking ahead, and saying too much. He may know where Luke's working. He may even know what name he's using. But even without that, this is great information we can give Malcolm…and Danny and Jim."

"Well, I'm sure if I tried to call back he wouldn't answer the phone," Martha said. "So what do we do now?"

"I'll call Malcolm." *He may not be too happy with me, but we accomplished something important.* "I need to let him know right away what we've found out."

To her relief, Malcolm didn't sound annoyed when Augusta told him about the phone call. "Martha had a letter from Bobby that she threw away. But in his letter, he told her the name he's been using since he left WITSEC—Benedetto Conti. He also told her he'd been auditioning at different opera companies. And he gave her his phone number, which she didn't write down for obvious reasons. I guessed he might have contacted the San Francisco Opera company. Luckily, he had, and they gave me his number. I'm sure he wouldn't have talked to me, and wasn't Martha great to make the call?" She smiled at her daughter-in-law.

"I'll be right there. I need to hear more," Malcolm said.

Martha put on coffee. "You've done this kind of thing before, haven't you?"

"Yes, I have. I usually manage to get some information that's helpful. Thanks again for helping me this time."

She wasn't sure what frame of mind Mal would be in when he arrived. But he was pleasant, though professional, when he came through the door. Maxie ran to hug his "Grandy" and wanted to show off his piano skills. Mal spent a few minutes with him until Martha turned "Sesame Street" on the living room television for her little boy. She served coffee for the adults in her dining room.

"I know you haven't 'Sesame Street'," she told them, "It's a brand-new children's show, and we all love it. It includes live actors interacting with life-size puppets, and it teaches so many great life lessons. And it uses a lot of music. Maxie loves it."

"Sounds interesting," Mal commented.

"However, that's not why you're here," Martha apologized. "Tell me how I can help."

"What name did you say Bobby is using?"

"Benedetto Conti. It kind of surprised me that he didn't change it completely, or maybe use a German or French name. But I guess that 'Ponti gene' is very strong," Martha said. "I had the phone on speaker so Augusta could hear him."

Mal nodded approvingly. "You didn't mention Vietnam. That could have aroused suspicion because of what happened to Luke there."

"No, Augusta and I wrote down what I should and shouldn't say. She told me the same thing you just did."

Augusta caught the half smile her husband gave her. *Oh, good. Maybe he won't kill me.*

"When I asked Bobby if his cousin was working in Cincinnati, his whole mood changed and he ended the conversation abruptly," Martha told Mal.

"It surprised me that Bobby may have realized Martha was fishing for information," Augusta said.

"Does he know she's married to a detective?" Mal asked.

"I did mention that I was married and we have a child," Martha answered. "And I said 'happily married.' I have to think he must keep in touch with someone who lives here, because he said he'd heard that I was married and still performing."

"So he might know you're married to my son," Malcolm said. "And if he does, he may have put two and two together and that's why he stopped talking."

Augusta folded her hands prayerfully under her chin. "Malcolm, Martha only did this because I suggested it. You can't begin to know how concerned I am about Allan. He seems to be dealing with this mess remarkably well, but I think that's a front. What if he's still under suspicion of murder and has to get up on stage before an audience of several thousand people and portray a villainous character? What would that do to him?"

"It's okay, Gus. I understand why you thought Bobby might be helpful to reach out to, and as it turned out, he was. And Martha, thank you for calling him and getting this valuable piece of information for us."

Augusta relaxed slightly as Mal continued, "However, Martha, keep in mind that this lady may be leading you down a primrose path. I'd suggest the next time she comes to you with some idea of helping investigate a murder, you check with Danny first."

"Copy that, Chief," Martha grinned and saluted.

Augusta, annoyed, folded her arms over her chest. "Primrose path? I sincerely doubt any harm was done, and now we have confirmation that Luke is right here under our noses. I think that's pretty darned important."

"Not so sure about the 'no harm done' part," Malcolm lifted an eyebrow. "We'll keep our fingers crossed that Bobby doesn't somehow find out about Allan's connection with Luke in Vietnam. That might create a problem."

Malcolm leaned back and gazed at Augusta, looking stern. "Did you not promise me recently you wouldn't even make a phone call without letting me know your plans?"

"Well…all I did was call the San Francisco Opera company to see if I could get Bobby's phone number," Augusta replied. "Or rather, Benedetto Conti's phone number. What harm could there have been in that?"

"Who knows? Did you use your real name and reason for asking about Benedetto?" Mal stared hard at Augusta, who didn't respond. "I didn't think so. Whatever alias you used, and wherever you pretended you were calling from…what if the person you talked to tried to call the Southern belle back?"

Augusta's mouth dropped open. "How did you know I used a Southern accent?"

Mal grinned. "Thought so. I know you've done that before." He took a final gulp of his coffee. "Next thing is to show our 'doctored' photos of Luke to Allan and find out if he's seen anyone around who resembles one of the pictures. Even if he hasn't, we get copies made up and give them to beat cops in strategic locations. Allan's neighborhood, Leslie's neighborhood. Places Allan frequents. The Conservatory, Music Hall, the VFW post. He may have other locations to suggest."

"When are you planning to do that?" Augusta asked.

"No time like the present," Mal replied as he stood. "Is Allan still at Milly's?" Augusta nodded. "Meet me there in an hour. I have to run back to the station and I want to bring Danny into this."

Martha walked her mother-in-law to the door. "You know what? I understand why you like to try to help with a case, especially one you're close to. I remember the first one...when Linnea Murphy was murdered." She smiled. "I'm sure you didn't think about it, but every student in the cast and crew of *The Pirates of Penzance* was betting on whether you were involved with Detective Mitchell."

"So the cast and the crew were gossiping about a possible romance between their director and the homicide detective? What did you think?"

Martha laughed. "Oh, there was no doubt in my mind. I saw how you looked at each other."

Chapter Fourteen
Multiple Identities

Wednesday, March 11

Later that afternoon

Mal spread out six photos on Milly's dining room table and asked, "Have you seen any of these men recently?"

Allan examined each one carefully, then pushed three back and pulled three closer. Of the photos he selected, one was of a man with longish hair, sideburns, and a moustache. One had shorter hair, sideburns, and a moustache, and the third showed the longish hair, sideburns, and no moustache.

They were all current styles that Augusta had seen on any number of young men, and she wondered how helpful the exercise might be.

Allan spent some time looking over each of the three photos. He rested a finger on the photo on the left. "This one. I'm sure I've seen this guy. But I have no idea where." He pushed the picture in the center into his other discards, and picked up the remaining photo.

"You know, this guy reminds me of Luke more. But I think if I'd seen him I might have wondered if it *was* Luke. If he's really trying to change his appearance…." He tapped his finger on the first photo. "That would do it."

Mal smiled. "That is in fact a photo of Luke Bridges as we imagined he would appear if he changed his look. And you believe you've seen him here."

"That confirms he's in Cincinnati, then? I'll have to thank Martha for being willing to call Bobby for that information." Allan frowned as he looked around at the detectives. "But how the hell can we find Luke in the next few days? I'm sure you can all understand I don't want this hanging over my head next weekend when I go out on stage."

Mal picked up the photos. "I'll have copies made of the photo you identified and pass them out to beat cops all over the city, especially in the areas where you spend time. And even in Newport, in case he's living there. We'll find him. If you can remember when and where you think you saw him, that would be helpful."

"I'll rack my brain, for sure. But you know, my preliminary hearing is tomorrow," Allan said.

"Garrett thinks he might be able to have it continued because of the important information Martha and Augusta uncovered. So that's a possibility," Malcolm replied. "And he believes it will eventually exonerate you."

"'Continued?' That doesn't mean 'case dismissed.' Believe me, I don't mean to complain—you all are doing so much for me and I will be eternally grateful—but I won't feel…I'm not sleeping well. And not just because of what I'm going through. I want to be able to offer Marissa support for what's happened to upend her life. And I want to be able to spend time with Les's parents. I know they'll be in town this weekend to take him home." He ran a hand over the back of his dark hair. "Sorry, guys, I don't mean to whine."

"It's okay, Allan, everyone understands the strain you're under," Mal responded, putting an arm on his shoulder. "One more thing: Since Bobby talked with Martha, there's a chance he may have contacted Luke…or a friend or family member…to let them know the CPD might be aware he's in the Cincinnati area. I believe it's unlikely, but to be on the safe side I'm assigning Jim Edmonds, Danny's partner, to stick close to you for the present. He'll pick you up and take you to Music Hall for tonight's rehearsal," Mal said.

"I really wanted to do that," Augusta said. "Can I meet Jim here, and he can follow us and park next to me? Allan and I use our driving time to discuss some aspects of his characters."

"No way," Danny said immediately, and Mal added, "I can't allow you to do that. Think about it."

Augusta gazed at him. *I'd be in danger as well, if Luke Bridges is still stalking Allan.* She nodded. "Sorry. Allan and I can talk before we leave for rehearsal."

Dan nodded. "Allan, we'll find Luke Bridges and bring him in for questioning. We can do that without checking in with the Sheriff's Office. From what we've learned it's possible he's still stalking you and may make an attempt on your life."

"If he is stalking you, that's a separate case and is taking place in Cincinnati. Now it's our case," Mal added.

Allan stared at them. "So if he's stalking me in Cincinnati…that means you can officially work on it, right? That makes me feel better."

***

Allan had his score open on his lap as he and Augusta sat in Milly's cozy library, enjoying the fire Garrett had built in the fireplace. Now that they were discussing his performance, Allan seemed more relaxed.

"I've really been looking forward to the staging of this act," he said. "In some ways, Dapertutto is the most interesting of these four characters. You know, something I read when I was first learning this…these nemesis characters are sometimes referred to as a shape-shifting demon. But I wasn't too sure about that. I know films have been made of the opera, but on stage, a tall guy is gonna be a tall guy."

Augusta nodded. "Yes, that's true."

"So I will need to present four different looks with makeup and wigs, and we've already selected the wigs. And the costumes will help as well. But mainly…it's attitude. How do I create these manifestations of a demon, if that's what the nemeses might be? As I said, I've been thinking most about this one. He fascinates me more than the others because evidently, he has no problem using his magical powers."

"Well, Dr. Miracle does as well. He's able to conjure up a vision of Antonia's dead mother."

"But he seems to limit himself to that. I think Dapertutto likes to...well, *play* with the people he bewitches. Giulietta in particular. I'm convinced he's her lover, and has such a strong hold over her she will do anything he asks. But he does it with a certain amount of charm. Evil charm."

"You've obviously already given this a lot of thought." Augusta was impressed. "Let's see what happens in this rehearsal. Of course, George is still filling in for Hoffmann, so your scenes with him won't be complete until the dress rehearsal when Jamie Logan is here."

"Hoffmann is secondary to Giulietta, so far as Dapertutto is concerned. He just wants his soul."

"Oh, is that all?!" Augusta laughed.

Allan leaned toward her, eager to share his ideas. "Dapertutto and Hoffmann don't interact much, because Giulietta acts on Dapertutto's behalf. Giulietta, on the other hand...I think in his own demonic way he loves her. He has complete control over her. Claudia and I discussed this." Claudia Prince, in addition to appearing as the ghost of Antonia's mother, had been cast as Giulietta—a role she told Augusta she was thrilled to perform. "We've rehearsed their scenes together."

Allan grinned. "In most productions they seem almost confrontational. We'd like to change that a bit...and make it more apparent they're lovers."

All of this was news to Augusta. "I had no idea you'd been working together on staging. Of course I'm eager to see what your ideas are." *I wonder if they're seeing each other? Is there something between them? They've kept it quiet if that's the case.*

"We tried a lot of things…and I admit, we had to tone it down some. I'm sure you'll let us know if you think what we'd like to do is a bit much."

"Well…Dapertutto is still the creature in charge of everything that happens," Augusta said.

"Oh, we know that. Why don't you take a look at our ideas and of course, if you don't like them…well, then, you don't like them. You are the actual one in charge," he said with a smile.

Augusta chuckled. "My goodness, that's a relief to know."

Jim had arrived, and Augusta drove to Music Hall thinking over Allan's ideas. Glancing in her rearview mirror she noticed they were right behind her.

Since she had the full cast for this act with the exception of Jamie, Augusta first gave directions to the ensemble. They took a break as she worked with the principals in the act. She had to admit Claudia and Allan had worked this out well. While this was a more sensual connection between Dapertutto and Giulietta, it was still apparent he was pulling all the strings.

Another short break for the principals, and Augusta called the full cast to the stage to do what she referred to as a "stumble-through." It was surprisingly anything but that. The entire cast seemed to catch the intensity of what Allan and Claudia were presenting, and it became more polished than Augusta expected. Even George had memorized this act and sang without a score. Augusta reminded him to make notes after the rehearsal to pass on to Jamie Logan.

The chemistry between Allan and Claudia gave the act heightened intensity. It began with Allan singing "Shine, Diamond, Shine," in which Dapertutto drew Giulietta to him with an enchanted jewel. Allan even provided a prop, a large fake diamond, and Augusta found his performance at least one of the best she'd ever experienced. It set the tone for the bewitched relationship between the two.

They touched briefly only a couple of times, but the connection between them—long glances, slightly outstretched hands, even turning the body at different angles—brought focus to their relationship. A strong moment occurred when Giulietta managed to steal Hoffmann's reflection into a magic mirror and triumphantly pass it on to Dapertutto. Augusta made a note to give to her lighting director to enhance that exchange with a light change.

She was acutely aware of how masterfully Allan performed this character. He was not the Allan Meissner she knew. He was an unearthly being holding reign over the people around him. *And with all he's dealing with in his personal life,* Augusta thought, *he's still able to do this. It's so real it's downright scary.* The act ended with Giulietta and Dapertutto exiting the stage together, intent on each other, without a thought for poor Hoffmann. Once again, Nicklausse/Irene was left to pick up the pieces for Hoffmann—but he did get his reflection back.

Augusta was delighted and thanked her cast for an excellent first stage rehearsal before she dismissed them.

As she packed her briefcase Augusta noticed Allan and Claudia off to one side, heads together, and then a warm embrace before Claudia left. *I believe they are together. She's a lovely woman, he' a good-looking guy. They have just about everything in common. She may be a few years older but I of all people don't see that as a problem,* she thought with a smile.

Back at Milly's, Garrett had left the fire burning, and it threw changing patterns on the walls in the library as Augusta and Allan discussed the rehearsal.

"Well, you made my job quite a bit easier," Augusta said. "I definitely appreciate all the work and thought you and Claudia put into this act."

"She's quite something," Allan said. "I guess you must realize we've been together...I mean, more than rehearsing."

"Claudia is lovely and I'm happy for both of you."

"It's very recent and I don't want to anticipate what might happen." He said. "But we're here to discuss the opera. This is my favorite act, even though Miracle is great to play as well. But Dapertutto...he's the man in charge. Or maybe the demon in charge." He paused. "What would it be like to have that kind of power? You know...if I were Dapertutto, I could find Luke Bridges—or anyone else—and do away with him like *that*." He snapped his fingers.

Augusta, a little startled, didn't laugh. "But you're not."

"No...I'm not. Too bad, isn't it?" Allan stared into the fire for a moment.

Augusta studied his face in profile. *What was it Milly said? Allan isn't living this role, he's acting it. But what if he has moved beyond acting? Is it at all conceivable that in some dark part of his mind—perhaps the part that was so affected by his experiences in Vietnam—he could possibly have...no...no, there's no way.* She shook her head slightly to banish the thought. *Get a grip, Augusta.*

Allan turned to her abruptly. "We need to call Malcolm. I just remembered where I saw the guy in the picture."

Susan Moore Jordan

Chapter Fifteen
"If you wrong us, shall we not seek revenge?"

11:15 p.m.

"I saw him in Union Terminal," Allan told them.

All three detectives and Augusta, Milly, and Garrett were seated with Allan around Milly's dining table. She had provided coffee and set out two trays of baked goods.

"My mother came to visit me over the Christmas holidays last December, and she took a train back to Baltimore because the weather wasn't good," Allan continued. "He was there. And he was dressed in a security detail uniform. So he's working at Union Terminal...or at least he was then."

"Well, if you saw him, chances are he saw you," Malcolm said. "My sense is he would have been surprised to see you there. In December he might have only recently arrived in town. And probably just started work at the station."

"I wasn't paying much attention because Mom and I were talking. Not sure why he caught my eye, but something about him...." He reached for a brownie.

Dan said, "Since we now know he's been here for several months and has made an effort to disguise himself...plus no doubt is living under an assumed name...it does seem our theory that he's the one who killed Captain Jerome and planted the murder weapon in your car when it was parked on the street is a logical explanation for this crime. While we can't charge him with that for obvious reasons—the murder case belongs to the sheriff—I believe we can pick him up on suspicion of stalking you and interrogate him." He looked to his father for confirmation, and Mal nodded in agreement.

"This will be tricky," Jim observed. "He's in a great place to make a quick getaway if he chooses to do that. Trains headed out of Cincinnati all the time, in every direction imaginable."

"We'll have to wait until tomorrow when the offices open to get Luke's phone number and address. But I can run down there earlier, say at seven, with the photo and talk to Sandy in the Box," Dan suggested.

"Sandy in the Box? Who in the world is that?" asked Augusta.

"A CPD patrolman whose beat is Union Terminal. William Sandoz has been on assignment in Union Terminal for decades. There's a small guard shack inside the terminal and that's why he's become known as 'Sandy in the Box,'" Dan explained. "He knows every inch of that building and every person who works there. He could confirm that Luke is working there."

Mal nodded. "Good suggestion. Go with it."

"Should we have a detail in the station at some point?" Jim asked. "Probably not tonight, if we're being careful not to tip him off. But maybe in the morning?"

"I'll put one together tonight and alert them to be ready tomorrow morning at any time," Mal said.

Garrett leaned forward. "Allan, you and I will go to the courthouse for the preliminary hearing as planned. I haven't yet had word about the continuance and Judge Demarest may be waiting for the hearing to give me his ruling on that. "

"I'm coming with you," Milly said.

"As am I," Augusta chimed in. "If Allan is comfortable with us being there."

"I appreciate the moral support," Allan said. "Garrett, what do you think will happen?"

"I think with any luck this situation will be resolved tomorrow. Maybe even before noon," Garrett replied. "We'll know more once our detectives have talked with the staff at Union Terminal, though."

"I suggest everybody try to get a good night's sleep," Malcolm said. "We need to be prepared for whatever tomorrow brings."

***

"A couple of things I've been wondering about," Augusta turned down the duvet on their bed. "Do you think Luke knew Leslie Jerome was in Cincinnati when he decided to come here? And why plant the murder weapon in Allan's car? Why not in his apartment?"

"Did Luke know that Jerome was living here when he decided to seek his revenge on Allan? Doubtful. I think it's likely he came here planning to murder Allan and saw Captain Jerome while he was stalking Allan. That gave him his idea to do away with both of them. As far as planting the gun in Allan's car—for one thing, it was much easier to break into his car and leave it there. If he'd gone to Allan's apartment, he would have had to know his schedule and Allan works irregular hours.

"And to get in, Luke would have needed to pick the lock. Not the easiest thing to do in an apartment building during the day when people are in and out, and risky at night especially with a veteran. For all he knew, Allan could be armed."

"Yes, all true. But you said 'for one thing.' Is there another reason?" Augusta removed her robe and settled into bed.

"He obviously made the anonymous phone call, tipping the police off to the murder weapon possibly being in Allan's car. Since one of Leslie Jerome's neighbors had seen Allan going into Jerome's apartment, the call was taken seriously and the cops were able to stop the car on a pretext and search it. Such a call wouldn't get the same result with a residence, because to search anyone's residence requires a warrant. And a warrant requires more evidence than what could be a crank call from a person who wants to get someone in trouble."

"You're suggesting Luke may have seen Allan go into Leslie's apartment building and waited until he left, then went into that building and got into Leslie's apartment and shot him."

Mal nodded. "He may have found Jerome's door unlocked. Or he might have picked the lock, if he had the right tools and knew how to use them."

"Have you talked to Leslie's neighbor…the one who claimed she heard loud voices coming from his apartment that night?" Augusta relaxed, her head on Malcolm's shoulder.

"I have not. I can't because it's not our case."

"What do you know about her, though?" Augusta asked.

"Her name is Miss Karen Peterson. I'm told she seemed quite interested in Leslie Jerome, even though she's in her fifties. She does seem to have been very much aware of comings and goings to his apartment, for whatever reason. It's unlikely she's a viable suspect."

"Why is that?"

"Of course, they checked her record. A couple of parking violations. An overdue parking ticket. One complaint of harassment from a former neighbor. Current neighbors rolling their eyes when asked about her. Not much reason to pursue her further."

Mal chuckled softly. "Garrett asked Allan about her saying she heard people yelling. He said when he was telling Leslie about the opera, he sang a few lines. He said to Garrett, 'That woman thought I was yelling? I must have been in really bad voice that night.'"

"I wish I could laugh, but I'm far too nervous about all of this," Augusta said. "Allan's rehearsal tonight was remarkable. It's amazing that he can put all this aside and completely immerse himself in Offenbach. Wait until you see him in this role."

"Impressive, is he?"

"I should say. He's spent a lot of thought on creating this otherworldly being...and I believe that's exactly what Offenbach intended with the character. Allan and I talked beforehand about the qualities of the four personalities he needs to present to the audience. Dr. Miracle is pretty scary because of the control he has over Antonia, and because he can summon up the spirit of her mother. But Dapertutto...."

"I remember you told me Allan's biggest aria is in that act. I recall he did a lot of singing in the Antonia act as well."

"Allan sees Dapertutto as a kind of demonic creature with the power to bewitch whomever he wants. Allan and Claudia had worked together on their scenes and showed me what they had come up with at our rehearsal. It's riveting. Allan's portrayal comes across as charming, but the charm covers who he really is. He has total control over Giulietta. You know...."

"Go on." Mal stroked her hair back from her face. "Sounds as if he is quite frightening in this act as well."

"Well, Dr. Miracle is bent on Antonia's death. Dapertutto just...*uses* people and tosses them aside when he's done whatever evil thing strikes his fancy. Like having Giulietta steal Hoffmann's reflection, which represents his soul. Allan was so convincing I actually had a momentary thought...." She paused.

"What? A thought that Allan might have murdered Captain Jerome? It surprises me you entertained that idea even for a second, Gus. Or were you aware of some conflict between the two men? Was Allan as nice about Leslie stepping in and winning Marissa Keyes' affections as we think he was?"

"I learned tonight Allan and Claudia have been spending time together and he told me it's gone beyond friendship. I had no idea until I saw them on stage. Which would seem to confirm he moved on from Marissa...but who knows? You're right, it's a crazy thought, but Allan's interpretation of Dapertutto's character is so convincingly evil—he believes he is all-powerful."

Mal rested his head on his hand. "So you wondered if someone might commit murder just because they believe they could get away with it? It's rare, but it happens. I could envision Luke Bridges doing exactly that. I can see members of organized crime families, including the Pontis, bumping people off on a whim. But otherwise, my take on that is a person would be mentally ill—or at least emotionally distressed—to commit such an act."

Augusta leaned on an elbow and gazed at Malcolm. "Such as suffering from severe trauma from being in Vietnam? And then being on stage playing the role of a shape-shifting demon?"

He kissed her softly. "Fortunately, the man you're speaking of is a good person and has close friends he knows he can share his emotional distress with. And perhaps even more...he has music."

Chapter Sixteen
An Unexpected Surprise

Thursday, March 12
9:30 a.m.

Allan's fingers shook as he attempted to adjust his tie. Milly moved closer to help him. "This may well all be over before you know it," she soothed.

"I don't know how I can perform next weekend if it isn't resolved soon." He caught a breath." I mean, I need to have the charges dropped and be completely exonerated."

Milly and Augusta exchanged a look, wondering how best to comfort their friend. Another pause, and Allan continued, "You can't know what this feels like. Being accused of murder. And the murder of a good friend."

The women both hugged him as they heard the phone ring. They all listened as Garrett responded, and hearing his end of the conversation made them aware something had happened that was not good.

Garrett turned to them as he hung up the phone. "I'm sure you realized that was Mal," he said. "Dan was at Union Terminal by seven and Sandy confirmed from the photo that Luke is working there. They know him as Larry Butler. Sandy said he started work just before Christmas, so it appears you did see him there when you took your mother to catch her train home, Allan." Garrett continued, "His co-workers aren't friendly with him. They think he's kind of an odd duck."

"No kidding," Allan said with a grimace.

"So what are the cops doing at this point?" Milly asked.

"Well, for one thing, Sandy called Mal and told him that Larry Butler didn't show up for work this morning. Sandy got his information from their employment office, and Luke, or Larry, who is living in the Over-the-Rhine neighborhood, is not answering his phone this morning. In the meantime, Mal has a detail waiting to head for the station, though if Luke isn't there I'm not sure there's any point in that."

"I would think Mal has sent either patrolmen or detectives to his home," Augusta commented. "He did say with what they've learned, they could bring him in for questioning."

Augusta noticed Jim had on the same expression she'd seen on Mal many times, what she considered his "full-on detective face." "You think this isn't good, don't you? The fact that no one knows where Luke Bridges is?"

Jim replied, "I'd feel better if we had some idea where he might be. We'll all stay on alert."

Augusta pulled Jim aside as Allan put on his jacket. "Will there be any other guards in the courtroom? I mean, in case…."

"Yeah, the bailiff. But there won't be any guards with Allan, because he's not being brought down from the jail. There will be the bailiff, me, and whoever Vogel sends over to testify." He paused. "I happen to agree with you that in these volatile times, armed guards in courtrooms would be a good idea."

Jim and Allan left for the courthouse as the other three prepared to follow in Garrett's car.

Such a peaceful day, Augusta thought. She glanced at Milly and Garrett, who appeared as tense as she felt. *So at odds with what we're all experiencing emotionally.*

"Could Luke know that Allan's preliminary hearing is this morning?" Milly asked, resting a hand on Garrett's arm.

"That's entirely possible," Garrett replied. "I'm sure there was a notice in the *Morning Call* today. I'm glad Jim's with us."

Augusta leaned forward. "Mal told me he hoped to have six patrolmen and two detectives on the detail for Union Terminal. That seems like a lot to just bring a man in for questioning."

"If he'd been at home, or was working his regular shift, it might be," Garrett replied. "But at this point we have no idea where he is. Mal's holding off on taking the detail over for now. If he *is* in Union Terminal even though he didn't report for work, and sees cops there, he might suspect they're after him, and that wouldn't be good. Especially if he decided to hide. You know how large the building is, but I doubt you have any idea how many places there are for someone to hide."

"I've only been in the main concourse, so no, I wasn't aware of that. I do know how large the building is," Augusta paused, thinking. "Let's not say anything about the possibility of Luke knowing about the preliminary hearing to Allan. He's under enough stress already."

A few minutes later they arrived at the courthouse where Jim and Allan were waiting for them outside. All five went inside, taking an elevator to the fifth floor. Garrett ushered them into a room to wait for the hearing.

Augusta realized Allan had become quiet. "This may be over much sooner than you realize," she comforted him. "Since Garrett will share with the judge what we've learned, your hearing may be postponed and hopefully Mal and his men will find Luke soon."

"And in that case, charges against you will undoubtedly be dismissed," Milly added.

Allan didn't appear reassured. "Or maybe not. Maybe Luke has already skipped town. It wouldn't surprise me."

"Let me check and see where we are with your court appearance," Garrett left the room. He returned almost immediately, looking none too pleased.

"Dan was just here. He tells me the police he sent to Luke's apartment in Over-the-Rhine found the door open, and the apartment had been cleaned out."

"That's bad," Allan said immediately, sitting down abruptly. "He's already left town. This is hopeless."

A tap on the door. Garrett answered, and turned to Allan. "The judge is ready to see us, but I'll speak to him privately in chambers first—in his office. The fact that we now know Luke Bridges has been living here under an assumed name, and is obviously now trying to get out of town, should convince him to at least postpone your hearing."

Augusta put a hand on Allan's back as they went into the courtroom. "This will all be over soon, I'm convinced of that," she said softly.

Garrett joined them and they waited for Judge Demarest to enter the courtroom. Augusta had a bad feeling about something though she wasn't sure what. Jim seemed unusually on edge. *Had Dan told him something that is making him extra alert?* Jim had a close eye on the courtroom door, and as she watched he unbuttoned his jacket and folded his arms over his chest so his right hand would be closer to the gun in his shoulder holster.

This is definitely not good, Augusta thought, trying hard not to communicate her unease to Milly and Allan.

Inside the courtroom, a number of people huddled in small groups, and Augusta surmised they were there for a similar purpose, for either an arraignment or a preliminary hearing. She recognized the bailiff and the court clerk; she recalled seeing them at other hearings she had attended. Garrett stood next to Allan, doing his best to keep him calm. Jim was on high alert; one hand near the radio on his belt, the other on his chest near his gun.

The first case on the docket was Allan's. The courtroom quieted. Just as the bailiff prepared to call the case, the hallway door flew open and a man stood framed in the entry, pointing a gun directly at Allan.

Even though he had changed his appearance again, Augusta knew it was Luke Bridges.

"Meissner!"

Allan whipped around to face the gunman and in that instant, Garrett leaped in front of him, collapsing as a bullet struck him. Jim got off a shot, but his bullet hit the door as it slammed shut behind Bridges.

Catching Garrett as he fell, Allan gently lowered him to the floor and quickly removed his jacket and shirt, searching for the wound site. Milly gasped and ran to Garrett—who was conscious but obviously in shock and now bleeding profusely—dropping on her knees next to him. As the judge hastily left the room, the bailiff ran to Garrett and knelt beside him. "Go, go, go get him," he hissed to Jim. "I've got this. I was a combat medic in Korea."

Jim ran from the room, yelling over his shoulder, "Someone call an ambulance!"

Ripping her cotton half slip off from under her dress, Augusta thrust it at the bailiff, who used it to apply pressure to the gunshot wound Allan had found in Garrett's left shoulder.

Augusta knelt and wrapped her arms around Milly, who tried in vain to muffle her sobs. Surprised, Augusta realized no one was screaming, there was just a rustle among the people in the courtroom. *Nobody has any idea what to do,* she thought.

She watched Allan help the bailiff apply pressure as they attempted to stanch Garrett's bleeding.

Oh, God, please don't let Garrett die.

Chapter Seventeen
Union Terminal

Jim sprinted to his car and headed for Union Terminal, talking to Malcolm on his radio as he drove.

"Big news, Mal. Bridges showed up just before Allan's hearing started," he said. "He shot at Allan but Garrett jumped in front of him and took the bullet. Bridges took off immediately. The bailiff told me he was a combat medic in Korea and started working on Garrett. I headed out as quick as I could. Ran down the steps, which I figured is what Bridges did."

"My God. How badly was Garrett injured?"

"Hard to say. Allan caught him before he hit the floor. Judging by the blood—and there's lots of it—the shoulder or upper chest. Here's some more news, Bridges has changed his appearance back. Clean-shaven, short hair, almost exactly like the picture your Marine buddy sent us. Dressed in dark blue slacks and a medium blue tweed sports jacket, white turtleneck shirt. Dark blond hair. Five-eleven, one-sixty. I got to the courthouse doors just in time to see him jumping into a cab. So his car isn't here. Maybe he parked at the train station."

"I doubt it's here either, but we can search the lots." Mal thought for a moment. "Sounds to me he may come down here, though, to grab a train and head out of town. He'll blend in with hundreds of other travelers. *Damn.*"

Mal heard car horns as Jim sped past other drivers, racing to get to Union Terminal.

"I'm already here at the terminal," Mal said. "Dan's at CIS waiting any further orders. I'll call in all the patrolmen we can get and have Dan round up all the detectives still in the unit. I'll also have him get copies made of the original photo and get those down here."

"It would be pretty bold of Luke to go to the terminal," Jim said. "If you don't think his car is there, where do you suspect it might be?"

"Outside of Cincinnati somewhere. Probably west of the city. He can get on a train headed in that direction, collect his car and head out to Vegas."

"I'm here," Jim said. Mal heard the car door slam. "Meet you at Sandy's Box?"

***

The ambulance arrived more quickly than Augusta had anticipated, and paramedics took over from the bailiff and Allan. Milly went in the ambulance with Garrett to General Hospital, first giving Augusta the keys to Garrett's car. After the frenzied activity getting Garrett out of the room there was confused calm. The bailiff went to speak with Judge Demarest.

Someone had the presence of mind to miraculously produce an abundance of wet paper towels. Augusta and Allan attempted to wipe the blood from their clothing and Allan's hands and arms, but didn't make much headway.

"Judge Demarest has requested me to advise you that your business with this court will be rescheduled and you will be contacted tomorrow as to when you should appear," said the bailiff in a formal tone, trying to inject some sense of normalcy into a courtroom that had been sent into turmoil in an instant. Augusta had to choke back a nervous giggle: his appearance and his announcement did not jibe in any way.

Augusta and Allan ran to Garrett's car. The drive to General Hospital took only minutes and neither of them spoke. *If he even survives the surgery, what's this going to do to him?* Augusta wondered. They parked in the emergency lot and hurried inside, drawing stares from onlookers. A nurse came toward them quickly and motioned for them to follow her.

"Mr. Stoddard is already in surgery," she told them. "Miss Devereaux is waiting in his private room and would like you to join her. There's a bathroom, you can clean up there. I'll bring extra towels."

Milly, seated by the bed, her hands folded on her lap, stood when they entered. Augusta ran to her and embraced her for a long moment. Allan remained by the door, unsure of what to do until Milly motioned to him to join them.

"Milly...I...," he stammered.

"Allan Meissner, don't you think for one second that any of this is your fault," Milly firmly told him as she embraced him. "How on earth could any of us have dreamed Luke Bridges would come to the courthouse today?"

Thank you, Milly, Augusta thought, as both women pulled Allan closer. Augusta was sure Milly recalled their conversation with Garrett as they drove to the Courthouse. *How can she be so calm?*

The nurse appeared with towels and extra soap, and Augusta said to Allan, "You first."

"Well…are you sure?"

She nodded, and he went into the bathroom, closing the door behind him.

"How bad?" Augusta asked.

"Very bad, Augusta…." Her voice wavered for an instant, but she quickly regained her composure and continued, "They rushed him into surgery the minute we came into the emergency room. Shoulder wounds can be deadly, you can bleed out so quickly. I don't believe I knew that, but Garrett has lost a lot of blood. I was told they would do everything they could to save his life." She was speaking in a low voice, and glanced toward the bathroom door. "Allan doesn't need to hear that. I'm sure he blames himself for this."

Allan came through the door, considerably cleaner than he had been, and wearing a clean set of scrubs the nurse had thoughtfully provided. He gazed at the two of them. "You're both being incredibly kind, but the truth is…if it weren't for me, Garrett wouldn't have been shot.

I can't believe he stepped in front of me. I should be the one in surgery right now."

"This is a great hospital, and the surgeon who is operating on Garrett is extremely skilled," Milly said. "I have faith that he's going to pull through. Allan, and you should, too."

She turned to Augusta. "Go on and get cleaned up. Allan will hold my hand."

***

Mal, Jim, and the original detail of six patrolmen and two detectives stood near Sandy's Box as he gave them the run-down on Union Terminal, a building he most likely knew better than anyone. He looked a little skeptically at the men, counting heads.

"Is this all the manpower you've got?" he asked Mal.

"Dan's bringing another detail over as soon as they all get to CIS. Twelve more patrolmen and another dozen detectives, so that brings us up to a total of thirty-two, plus Jim, Dan and myself."

"If your guy is hiding in this building, here's what you'll be dealing with." Sandy ticked off items on his fingers as he shared them. "There are four vehicle entrances and exits on the main level. There are dozens of, maybe even a hundred exits inside the structure on the Dalton Street level and the main level, all the way west down to the end of the concourse to the trains."

Sandy looked around at the men to be sure they were paying attention. "And that's just the places the public is allowed. If you open any one of several dozen doors you find yourself in stairwells that go up to the six levels of offices in the outside of the rotunda. You could even walk across the front of the terminal on glass sidewalks at any of the six floors."

"That's a lot," Jim commented.

"Wait, I'm not done yet," Sandy said "If you found your way up above the ceiling of the rotunda, there's a superstructure of girders and at least thirty feet to the roof and many places to hide."

Mal and Jim exchanged glances as Sandy added, "Then there are the lower levels, including the morgue. You could bring the whole CPD down here and not find him!"

Mal carefully considered what should be done before speaking: "Maybe best to have the uniforms at the main floor stairways to the upper floors. I don't think he's come here to hide, but if he's up there, he will be pinned up there. We'll also put some uniforms at strategic positions outside where they can see all the exits on the ground level. For the detectives, we need to make some educated guesses. One, I think Luke is here to escape on a train. Two, I think he's going west. Let's assign one detective to the Operational Control Center and split the others up among the passengers of the westbound trains."

Dan and the additional detail arrived on the scene, and Mal quickly filled them in on the plan. Jim took the photos and passed them out. "He'll no doubt figure out we're looking for him. If you spot Bridges, keep track but call one of us immediately and try to stay with him."

***

Augusta was somewhat shocked to see herself in the mirror. She didn't recall touching her face or hair at the courthouse while she was helping care for Garrett, but blood was on her forehead and hair as well as hands and arms. She scrubbed her face, neck, hands, and arms, used a wet towel on her hair and managed to remove most of the blood.

Milly is amazing. She seems so calm, and that's exactly what Allan needs. I guess it's what I needed as well.

Augusta took off her dress and eyed it. She had found the scrubs the nurse brought for her. Spreading out her dress, she thought, *Garrett's blood. I'll never be able to wear this dress again, even if it could be cleaned.* She threw it on the pile of soiled towels on the floor, quickly donned the scrubs, and rejoined Milly and Allan.

Some thoughtful staff person had brought in cold drinks and snacks for Milly and her friends, and Augusta gratefully took a long drink of hers. *I didn't realize I was so thirsty.* She glanced through the window. "Wonder what Mal and his men are doing? Of course they're after Luke, and perhaps they've even caught him already."

"I seriously doubt that," Allan replied. "I'm still processing this—that he wanted me dead to the extent he'd come to the courthouse and try to kill me. I don't know a lot about how members of organized crime think, but I'd guess he had his getaway planned."

Augusta didn't know how to respond, but she thought back on her experiences with this particular organized crime family and had to agree with Allan. "Maybe. I think the best thing we can do is pray for Garrett. He's in a great hospital, I'm sure he has the best surgeon on the staff operating on him, and he's strong and in excellent health."

They all fell silent. Augusta understood; what else was there to say?

Find the S.O.B., Malcolm, and make sure he spends the rest of his life locked up.

Chapter Eighteen
You Can Run, But You Can't Hide

12:15 p.m.

While not the bustling travel hub it had been at one time, Cincinnati's Union Terminal still served hundreds of passengers daily and had also become a point of interest for many tourists. Built during the 1930s, it boasted the largest half-dome in the Western Hemisphere. The imposing art deco mosaic murals, depicting industries in the city, inspired awe in the tourists and travelers who took the time to admire them.

Mal's strongest memories of the times he had spent in this station were during the Second World War. He had left his family and city from here, and it was to this terminal he and thousands of other veterans returned. The terminal had been at its busiest during that era, serving more than sixty thousand travelers daily.

Now Mal stood for a moment with Jim and Dan. They had deployed their troops and the three of them were to join the westbound travelers and mingle, hoping to find and arrest Luke Bridges before he could board a train.

Hearing Sandy talk about the immensity of the building was one thing, but as they stood in the concourse, Mal had a moment where he felt outside of himself, an almost overwhelming sense of the enormity of what they were dealing with. He stared up into the vastness above them. *Sandy's right, Bridges could completely disappear.* The voice of the announcer brought him back into the bustle of the concourse.

"I don't like this," Mal said, watching the travelers moving quickly toward the tracks. "The last thing I want is for a civilian to be hurt because we're after a criminal and may have to use force. I know I don't need to say it, but no guns if there is any way to avoid even showing them."

Jim said, "I think I shouldn't be too close to you, Chief. I saw Bridges, and I'm sure he saw me. I'll try to stay in the background as much as I can until I'm needed."

Mal nodded. "Keep an eye out and stay where at least one of us can see you."

"Visual signal?" Jim asked.

"No, let's use our radios," Mal responded, inserting his earplug. They separated and joined the throng headed toward the westbound trains. Mal a few steps behind Dan, Jim joining the passengers further back but still within eyeshot.

Sounds of a busy train station echoed through the building: announcements of departing and arriving trains, happy sounds of families going on a trip, people calling out to friends and family just arriving in Cincinnati. The three detectives moved toward a train they knew was departing in the next ten minutes for Indianapolis, acting on Mal's hunch that Bridges had somehow situated his car near that city the day before.

Mal glanced across the terminal to see his uniformed patrolmen holding their positions. A few travelers glanced at them, but most didn't even seem to realize there were more cops than usual in the building. As they drew closer to the tracks, the crowds and the noise grew substantially. Baggage handlers joined the throng.

The number of civilians who might be in danger was of real concern to Mal. He and his detectives would only shoot if absolutely necessary, but he had no control over what Bridges might do. *I hope he's not stupid enough to try to grab a hostage if it comes to that,* Mal thought. *On the other hand, he was stupid enough to shoot a man in the Hamilton County Courthouse. All bets are off with this guy.*

They neared the train, searching faces in the throng as they moved forward. *This is like looking for a needle in a haystack,* Mal thought. *I hope my hunch was right.*

Suddenly he heard Dan's voice in his earpiece: "Target dead ahead, four or five steps." Mal relayed the information to Jim. As Dan and Mal moved more quickly to close in on their perp, they both saw their opening and in a few steps had him between them. Dan put a hand on Bridges' chest and took his elbow. "Mr. Bridges, you have to come with us. Let's do this peacefully, sir."

It surprised Mal how quickly and easily this had taken place. Luke was apparently so intent on boarding the train he never had a thought that the police might be in hot pursuit.

But it wasn't to be quite that easy. Bridges jerked away from Dan, turned and saw Mal, and reached into his pocket. Mal grabbed his wrist and twisted it hard. People around them moved away, confused. A few gasped and one let out a startled scream.

Bridges yanked his gun from his pocket to more screams from onlookers. Mal twisted Luke's wrist with both hands, throwing him off balance. Bridges fell hard on one knee and dropped the gun. He managed to jerk himself upright as he wrenched free from Mal's grip, and started to run. Mal, pursuing him, gun drawn, heard more reactions from the onlookers as they hustled out of his way. Parents protected their children with their bodies.

Glancing back over his shoulder, Luke ran straight into Jim, who had his gun drawn. "On your knees, Bridges," he ordered as Luke stopped short. More gasps from people close to the action.

Two other detectives ran into the group and helped Jim and Mal subdue Bridges, bringing him to his knees, as Dan quickly retrieved the gun, using his handkerchief to handle it. Jim slapped handcuffs on Luke and yanked him to his feet as he said, "You're under arrest for the attempted murder of Garrett Stoddard."

Displaying his shield, Mal said loudly, "Police. Everything's fine, folks. Please just give us some room here."

The three detectives, Jim and Dan on each side of Luke and Mal behind them, took their captive back through the terminal and past Sandy's Box.

Sandy stared at Luke. "Well, I'll be damned. Even if he walked right past me when he came in, I doubt I would have recognized him," he marveled.

"Let the detail know it's all over," Mal said, as the detectives headed for the exit with their prisoner.

***

Back at Criminal Investigations Section, Mal found Herb Vogel, Chief of Detectives for the Sheriff's Office, waiting to see him.

"First, I hear Garrett Stoddard was shot at the courthouse while he was there for Allan Meissner's preliminary hearing. Next, I hear about a big police detail at Union Terminal and a guy being arrested for shooting somebody. I figure that 'somebody' must have been Attorney Stoddard. I also know that Stoddard was rushed to General Hospital and into surgery but is still alive. Why do I have a feeling this may have something to do with the murder of Leslie Jerome?"

"Because it does. The man we arrested, Luke Bridges, is very likely the man who killed Captain Jerome and planted the murder weapon in Meissner's car. Have a seat and I'll tell you the whole story."

Mal proceeded to go back to the incident in Vietnam, Bridges' threats being reported to Allan, and Luke's eventually coming to Cincinnati to make good on the threat. "We're sure someone in the Bridges-Ponti

165

crime family let Luke know we were on to him, and that's when he decided to take his revenge by killing Allan himself instead of waiting to see if the State of Ohio would do it for him. Dan is contacting the Shelbyville PD to see if they can find his car. My hunch is he drove it over to Indiana last night, got a cab to bring him back here and then planned to take a train headed for Indianapolis today after he murdered Allan Meissner. I learned Shelbyville is frequently a short stop for the through train to Indy, so he could grab his car and drive out to Vegas."

"This guy who told Meissner about Bridges' threats...is he available to testify?" Vogel asked.

"I don't know why he wouldn't be. We'll have Allan contact him, and 1 would think it likely he will testify. And maybe a notarized statement or a taped interview will suffice?" He leaned back. "I know you had the pistol, but no corroborating evidence. And I've learned recently that Allan Meissner is in a relationship with another woman, so the 'love triangle' motive doesn't hold water."

"Well...we also have a stack of letters a foot high from people offering to be a character witness for Meissner. A lot of the vets at the VFW. People he knows through his musical activities. Father Dennis Halloran was the first person we heard from." He grinned. "Oh, and a lady you probably know. Professor Augusta McKee."

Mal smiled wryly. "That doesn't surprise me, but she hadn't told me she did that."

"Sounds as if we arrested the wrong guy." Vogel stood. "Though finding the gun in his car was pretty damning."

"Yes, it was. Can we arrange to meet with the prosecutor and ask to have the murder charge against Meissner dropped? Then we can pursue that charge against Bridges instead, along with the attempted murder of Stoddard." Mal stood and the men shook hands.

"What do you hear about Stoddard?"

"Nothing yet, so it could become another murder charge. I want to call the hospital and find out how he is, and then I need to interrogate Luke Bridges."

It eased Mal's mind to learn from General Hospital that Garrett had survived surgery and was now listed in critical but stable condition, which he knew meant Garrett's vital signs were strong but he was still unconscious.

Danny came into his office. "Martha called," he told his father. "Augusta contacted her about Garrett and how she was at the hospital, so she and Maxie went to your house to take care of Fritz. She said she'd wait there until she heard more. Augusta also said she has plenty of toys and snacks available, as you no doubt know. They can stay as long as we need them to."

"Good to know. And yes, a box of toys behind the sofa in the living room. We always have enough snacks for at least two little kids. There's plenty of real food on hand as well."

Mal stood as he picked a pad and pen. "Let's go talk to Mr. Bridges, shall we?"

Chapter Nineteen
The Best-Laid Plans

Thursday, March 12
5:00 p.m.

Mal watched his killer through the one-way mirror as Luke Bridges looked around the interview room. *I wonder what he's thinking. He's got to know he's toast at this point.*

A tap on the outside door and Danny opened it. "The Shelbyville PD called. You were right, they found Larry Butler's...or rather, Luke Bridges'...car, packed with essentials and fully gassed up. You were spot on about his plans."

"Yeah. A little scary, isn't it?" Mal grinned. "I guess when you deal with bad guys as much as I have, you start to think like they would when they're cornered. I still find it tough to believe he actually thought he'd get away with this, though."

"Well, for one thing, he had no idea we knew what he looks like now. So even if an alert was issued with a description, he wouldn't be that visible," Dan said. "And he probably thought the search would be confined to the Greater Cincinnati area, which is why he wanted to get on that one o'clock train to Indianapolis."

Gripping his file folder, Mal entered the interview room. Bridges sat up as straight as he could, his range of movement limited by his left wrist being handcuffed to a chair leg.

Mal pulled a chair up opposite him, opening the folder. "You know, Luke, you shoot a guy in front of a room full of people and most of them are going to remember you."

"I was acting on behalf of my commanding officer in Vietnam. Allan Meissner murdered Captain Leslie Jerome."

Oh, so that's your defense? "Even if that were true, revenge homicide is not a legal defense in this day and age. You know that."

"I couldn't let him get away with what he did. Captain Jerome didn't deserve to die." Luke leaned forward, staring Mal in the eyes.

What's he doing, trying to work up an insanity plea of some kind? "Cut the bullshit, Bridges. We know exactly what happened in Vietnam, and we know you ended up serving jail time for it. We also know, and I believe we can prove, about your threats to both Captain Jerome and Allan Meissner."

"I have no idea what you're talking about." Luke leaned back, continuing to stare into Mal's eyes. "I want a lawyer. I called my family and they're providing one for me. I don't have to talk to you."

"Maybe not, but I think you need to listen to what I have to say." Mal leaned toward Bridges. "You came to Cincinnati under an assumed name, altering your appearance. Hardly heroic, wouldn't you say? You stalked both Leslie Jerome and Allan Meissner, and eventually you shot Jerome in his apartment and then planted the gun in Meissner's car. Then you made an anonymous phone call to the Elmwood Place police and told them they could find the gun there. You must have been pretty convincing, because they investigated the tip."

Bridges carefully kept any emotion from showing on his face. *He's good*, Mal thought. "A couple of things, though, you didn't consider. There are those here in Cincinnati, and in our law enforcement contingent, who have dealt with your family and understand how they operate. A phone call to one of those family members confirmed you were here in Cincinnati."

A frown from Bridges, who otherwise remained impassive. "I said I want to wait for my lawyer."

"And that's your right. I'm just talking to you, Luke. I'm not asking any questions. I'm just giving you some information I believe you need," Mal said mildly.

"We made a guess as to how you might have changed your appearance." Mal shoved a copy of the photo across the table. "When Meissner saw this, he recognized you. He recalled seeing you in Union Terminal, wearing a uniform. The same uniform he saw on other Union Terminal employees."

A muscle began to twitch in Luke's cheek.

Mal closed the file. "What I don't get is why you didn't just get of town then? Why shoot Meissner? I have to ask myself if you hate him that much that you tried kill him in front of a courtroom with over a dozen witnesses."

Luke looked away. Mal noticed a drop of perspiration slide down the side of his face. *Not quite as cool as he'd like to be. Time for the coup de grâce.*

"Here in Ohio, premeditated murderers go to the electric chair. There is no more crystal clear premeditation than all the planning you did to kill Jerome and frame Meissner." He glanced at his folder.

"Then you try to kill Meissner. Again, premeditated. All the way to planning your escape. Oh, and yes, we found your car in Shelbyville, which of course makes it an interstate flight to avoid prosecution and therefore possibly a federal case." *The twitching is worse. I'm getting through.*

Mal continued, "You shot and probably killed an officer of the court, a Hamilton County court. The same court before which you will be tried. There will be no asking for mercy in that court. You may get the trial moved to another county, but no matter how far away it's moved, the stink of it will follow you."

Mal leaned forward. "Your attorney will tell you to say nothing, not a word. All through any appeals, all the time you'll be locked up waiting for trial. All those countless thousands of dollars of attorney fees. But here's something you need to think about while you're waiting to meet that high-priced attorney: if you admit to killing Captain Jerome and attempting to frame Allan

Meissner, there's a chance...a chance...the death penalty might be taken off the table."

A flicker in Luke's expression, but he didn't respond.

"In any event, you're spending the night in jail. You'll be arraigned in the morning." Mal stood, taking his time, but Luke still didn't speak.

Mal instructed the guard to secure the prisoner as he left the room. He motioned to Dan to follow and they went back to Mal's office.

"I called the hospital earlier," Dan said. "No change in Garrett's condition. Do you want to keep the patrolmen on duty there?"

"Just to be on the safe side, let's keep them overnight. I want to get over there and I don't know how long I'll stay. If Gus wants to stay with Milly, I'll keep her company." Mal put on his jacket, preparing to leave. "Can you get in touch with Martha? And maybe take Fritz to your place for the present?"

"Why don't I just go to your house and Martha and I can figure it out from there? Maxie's spent the night there before and I know Augusta has pajamas for him. I think she makes up a bed for him on the chaise, right?"

***

Mal wolfed down the food he picked up at Frisch's as he drove to the hospital. Before he headed for Garrett's room, he asked to speak with whoever was currently caring for Garrett. The physician on duty filled him in on exactly what had been done and told Mal, to his great relief, they were confident Garrett would recover.

Opening the door to Garrett's room quietly, he saw Milly sleeping in a chair, Allan in another, his long legs stretched out in front of him. Augusta stood when she saw Mal and motioned for him to follow her back into the hall.

He held her close for long moments as she clung to him. "There's a small waiting room down this hall," she said. "We can talk in there. Milly is exhausted. Allan is as well. It's good they both are getting some sleep."

"This must be extremely hard for Allan," Mal said.

"Yes, of course it is. Dennis was here earlier and I believe that was helpful, but Allan still blames himself for Garrett being shot."

"Have you had any food?"

"Yes, we all had dinner about five-thirty. What time is it, anyway?"

Mal glanced at his watch. "After eight. Dan went to our house and he and Martha may just stay overnight with Maxie. Probably easier than taking Fritz home with them."

"I should call Martha. There's plenty of food there."

"They'll figure it out, Gus." He brushed back her hair. "I talked to the physician on duty and Garrett is in good hands. He'll survive this."

She stared at him. "You know more than we've been told."

"It's because I'm a cop. Medical people generally talk to us differently. Especially in a case like this, with a criminal investigation for a gunshot wound."

"All I know is that a nurse comes in about every half hour and checks something. I guess the best thing is no doctors rushing in, no blinking lights or beeping sounds going off." She sighed, a sigh that seemed to him to come from the depths of her being.

Mal pulled her to the small sofa and they sat close. "Talk to me, Gus. I can tell something is really troubling you."

"Oh, Mal, if Garrett dies…."

"I honestly don't believe that's going to happen. Everything I've heard sounds positive, despite the emergency surgery when you first arrived. Or more likely, because of it."

"This is all my fault." Another sigh. "If I hadn't insisted that Martha call Bobby…he would never have contacted Luke and tipped him off that people knew he's in Cincinnati. Luke's a Ponti, he would have put two and two together and realized the cops were after him. And he wouldn't have shown up at the hearing and shot at Allan. And hit Garrett, who was such a hero."

She gulped hard, but the tears began to trickle down her face. "Why don't I listen to you when you tell me to stay out of your cases? It's too late for me to say it, but I'll never do it again." A sob. "If Garrett dies it's my fault. And I'll never forgive myself. Nor will poor Milly, my best friend…."

Mal pulled her close and let her weep. It had been an unbelievably stressful day. When she grew quieter, he lifted her chin.

"You know, I see this differently. First of all, we don't know for a fact that Bobby got word to Luke that we were on to him. It's entirely possible he may have realized on his own that his attempt to pin Captain Jerome's murder on Allan wasn't going to work, and decided to kill Allan and get out of town. I think you even mentioned that possibility once, that Bridges might kill Allan as well."

"Did I?" Mal saw a change in her expression and kept talking.

"You thought about the possible connection between Luke and Bobby and you decided we needed to know about it. You figured out how to find Bobby, who confirmed he knew Luke, and even let slip that Luke was here in Cincinnati. So now we had a workable theory and a suspect. That was a huge break in the case, Gus. Before that, it was just a vague idea that somehow Luke might be connected to Jerome's murder. And while we thought he could be here looking for revenge, we didn't *know* that. Once we knew for a fact he was right here under our noses, that changed everything."

"Yes, but…."

"And I know how much you've been concerned about Allan. If this case had dragged on, who knows what that might have done to him? How it would have affected his performance, the Met audition…his whole future?" He stroked her hair back from her face. "Who knows why Luke revealed himself and tried to kill Allan? His mind doesn't work the way ours does."

Mal smiled and again caressed her face. "You'll be glad to know this. I talked to Herb Vogel today. He agreed to drop the charges against Allan when I told him what we'd learned."

Augusta returned the smile. "That's wonderful." A muffled sigh. "But still…what a terrible shock to see Garrett shot, right there at the courthouse. All that blood…." She shuddered.

He kissed her cheek softly. "Give yourself a break, my love. I'm sure Garrett will recover. We have Luke in jail and he'll face punishment for what he did. And Allan is exonerated, thanks to you."

Augusta wrapped her arms around him and he held her close.

"Want to go back to Garrett's room?" He asked.

"Not really. Can you stay with me?" She smothered a yawn.

"That was the plan." He leaned back against the couch and pulled her close. "Why don't you try to relax…maybe even get some sleep?"

He held her gently and felt her relax as she drifted off to sleep, and before long they were both dozing comfortably.

Allan found them early the next morning. Kneeling next to the couch, he shook them gently. "Augusta. Malcolm."

They opened their eyes and gazed at him sleepily, surprised to see him smiling. "Garrett's awake. His doctor says he's out of the woods."

Chapter Twenty
The Show Goes On

March 20
7:30 p.m.

Backstage at Music Hall, Augusta spoke to her cast of *The Tales of Hoffmann*.

"*In bocca al lupo*, Jamie...*Bocca al lupo*, Claudia...Martha...," and each of them responded, "*Crepi...Crepi il lupo...Crepi....*" She loved seeing the excitement in their faces as they exchanged the traditional Italian expression wishing a singer luck, "In the mouth of the wolf" and the response, "May the wolf die," often shortened to a single word.

She had addressed the entire cast earlier, thanking them for sharing their talent and their love of music. Allan remained, and the moment they had together was one she would always remember.

"Be brilliant," she told him. "I don't need to wish you luck. I know what you can do with this role and I intend to love every minute."

He held her by the shoulders and gazed into her eyes. "My dear friend and mentor. There is no way I can ever thank you for everything you've given me. The best I can do is perform for you tonight, from my heart."

They shared a long embrace. They'd been through a war together and come out on this end, having won all the battles.

Augusta turned and blew a last kiss to her incredible cast before joining Malcolm at the stage door to find their way to one of Thomas Schippers' private boxes. He had generously given the use of it to Augusta for this opening night performance.

"Are you all set for tomorrow?" he asked.

"Yes, all the principals are delighted to help us out." Garrett, recently released from the hospital, could not attend the opera, and Milly didn't want to leave him. Augusta and Allan had spoken with cast members and arranged for a brief recital of some of the music at Milly's house the following morning. Thomas Schippers had agreed to play for them. "I love that Allan thought of taking the opera to Garrett, and that the singers were happy to participate."

"There's something special about this production, Gus," Mal commented. "Like walking through flame and coming out on the other side stronger."

"It does feel that way. Especially for Allan."

An excited Maureen Meissner, Allan's mother, waited in the lobby to meet them. Mal was struck by her small stature, as Augusta had been when they first met during Allan's undergraduate years. Augusta remembered her well, but she seemed even more attractive than she recalled. Allan had inherited her dark hair and eyes and her warm smile, though his height came from his father. They collected Maureen and found their way to the box, where they met Marissa Keyes, her parents, and Dennis Halloran. . Dennis had met Marissa when she began seeing Allan, and she turned to him as a counselor as she struggled with Leslie's loss. Dennis had met Maureen earlier and made introductions all around.

"How is Allan?" Maureen asked Augusta. "He didn't say much when we were getting ready to come here, and I sensed it was probably a good idea not to talk to him." She sounded a little anxious and Augusta patted her arm.

"You'll see," Augusta smiled. "I'm sure you have maternal jitters, but try not to. He was born to play this role."

Maureen laughed. "A villain? He's definitely playing against type."

"He has the ability to dig into his characters and understand what makes them tick," Augusta replied. "To say nothing of the vocal ability necessary to perform the nemesis successfully. As I said…you'll see. And Allan not wanting to talk? He was preparing himself mentally for this demanding role."

They settled into their seats, the hall darkened, and Maestro Schippers came to the podium. Soon the opening chords of Offenbach's masterpiece filled the hall. The curtains parted, and the first principal onstage was Irene as "The Muse of Poetry" explaining in a monologue who she was, and why she would be appearing as Hoffmann's companion Nicklausse in this story.

Allan entered as Lindorf and Augusta was pleased to hear the audience acknowledge him enthusiastically. A brief comedic scene followed with a messenger delivering a letter to Hoffmann that Lindorf intercepted. Allan's opening aria received prolonged applause.

They are with him, Augusta thought, tears in her eyes. *How perfect.*

Jamie Logan's entrance as the melancholy poet Hoffmann had the audience on their feet. The young tenor had been a graduate student at the Conservatory before beginning his career a few years earlier, and now was sought after worldwide. *To the Cincinnati audience, he will always be 'our boy,'* Augusta thought. It was a true thrill to hear him again, his brilliant tenor voice perfectly suited to this role.

After a brief pause for a fast scene change, the curtains opened on the "Olympia" act. Italian-American coloratura Sylvia Cabrini had proved to be a perfect Olympia. Petite and trim, with high notes even above standard coloratura range, Augusta understood from their first rehearsal why she was performing this role all over Europe. Allan's entrance as Coppelius was quasi-comedic and he sold a pair of "magic glasses" to Hoffmann, who then saw Olympia as a real woman rather than the automaton created by Coppelius and Spalanzani. Even though warned by Nicklausse, Hoffmann—as well as the audience—was totally bedazzled by Cabrini's Olympia. She performed the role of the doll perfectly while singing exquisitely.

When Coppelius returned to confront Spalanzani, he first showed the viciousness in the nemesis character. Since the bank draft for her purchase had been worthless, he claimed Olympia, taking her away and destroying her. Augusta loved the reaction of the audience to see the pieces tossed onto the stage with Coppelius appearing briefly one last time as Hoffmann finally realized the truth, that Olympia was a mechanical doll. While much of the act had been humorous, suddenly it became intense and shocking. Augusta had requested special lighting and Allan's shadow loomed across the stage.

During intermission, Augusta and her guests enjoyed a glass of champagne at the bar in the lobby. Several people stopped and spoke to Augusta, complimenting her on the production.

"I can't thank you enough for inviting us to join you, Augusta," Marissa said. "I hadn't realized how great box seats are. And what a treat to see Allan in this role. I know how hard he's worked on it."

Her parents turned to speak to friends and Marissa leaned closer to Augusta, saying sadly, "I wish Leslie were here. He would be so proud of Allan."

Augusta had to wait for a moment before responding, finding tears close to the surface. "I'd like to think he *is* here, Marissa. I believe the people we love never really leave us, in a way."

Marissa nodded. "Father Halloran said the same thing to me just yesterday. He's been such a help to me. So has Allan. I'll never find a truer friend." She managed a small smile. "Allan tells me you've taken some artistic license with this production, and he loves what you've done."

Augusta laughed. "Marissa, opera houses have been doing that almost since the opera was first available. Offenbach, sadly, didn't live to complete it. I think for one thing he'd have shortened the dialogue scenes, too, at least a bit. Everybody does that. But I also re-imagined the ending and added some drama in a few other spots. And Claudia and Allan made some great suggestions for the 'Giulietta' act. Maestro Schippers approved, and the cast seems to like it."

Marissa's mother spoke to her and she rejoined her parents. *I'm glad her parents are here to help her,* Augusta thought. *And it's wonderful that the three of them are here tonight to support Allan.*

The opening notes of the "Barcarolle" sounded through the lobby, performed by one of the orchestra's trumpet players to announce the end of intermission. Augusta felt Mal's strong hand under her elbow.

"Where did you disappear to?" she asked.

"Talking to the judge," he replied, referring to Edgar Demarest. "We were discussing why Luke Bridges decided to confess. The judge thinks it wasn't his decision. He feels sure it was 'the family' who told him to agree to plead guilty."

"Why would they do that?" Augusta said, genuinely surprised.

"Well, sure, that bunch bumps people off all the time, but it's usually members of other crime families. Or sometimes even members of their own families. They had no beef with Leslie Jerome. That was Luke's personal vendetta. They weren't going to spend big dough to pay for his defense. He was going to get convicted anyway. So, Luke is safely locked up in the Ohio State Penitentiary in Youngstown, and there he will end his days."

The curtain opened on the "Giulietta" act. Irene as Nicklausse and Claudia as the courtesan Giulietta sang the well-known and much loved "Barcarolle" as a duet, and it was then repeated by the full chorus. A lush, sensuous melody that enchanted, enhanced by stunning costumes and a beautiful, atmospherically lighted set, as Giulietta seduced and then abandoned Hoffmann at the urging of Dapertutto. Augusta sat entranced, watching her cast perform as she knew they would. It was what she had seen at their staging rehearsal, multiplied tenfold. It was perfection. She hardly breathed as she watched and listened. *I think Offenbach would approve.* At the end of the act, Allan as Dapertutto was the last person to exit the stage, his shadow again looming large as he watched Nicklausse drag Hoffmann away. Applause began slowly and grew to a huge roar when the act ended.

Maestro Schippers wisely gave the audience a few minutes to react and settle down before lifting his baton for the final part of the opera, the "Antonia" act. After the glamour and glitz of Venice in the previous act, the curtain opened on a simple but gloomily fantastic scene, a house in Munich. Heavily draped windows with violins hung on the walls. Martha as Antonia sat at a spinet piano, singing sadly.

Just listen to her, Augusta thought. *She fits right in with this high-powered cast. She could be a star rather*

185

than a mostly stay-at-home-mom, limiting her career to performing regionally. Well, this is her choice, her decision to make. It's wonderful for little Maxie. I'm just so happy she's performing this role.

Hoffman appeared and he and the ailing Antonia enjoyed a rapturous reunion, interrupted by her father, Crespel, and by the arrival of Allan as Dr. Miracle. Crespel had tried to hide Antonia from Hoffmann and from Dr. Miracle, whom he believed had "treated" and killed his wife by forcing her to sing, and whom he believed now wanted to kill Antonia.

Of all three acts, Augusta felt this one most showed Offenbach's genius. In one scene, after Antonia had been sent to her room, Hoffmann eavesdropped while Dr. Miracle worked his magic, appearing to lead an invisible Antonia toward him, represented by a light moving across stage. When Miracle ordered Antonia to sing, Martha's voice soared offstage, thrilling Augusta and she was sure everyone else. A favorite of Augusta's was the trio that accompanied part of this scene: Dr. Miracle, Hoffmann, and Crespel. She thought it some of the finest writing in the opera.

When Hoffmann learned if Antonia sang she would die as her mother had, he begged her never to sing again. But after Hoffmann left the house, Dr. Miracle continued to unleash his evil magic.

He called Antonia to him, raising the spirit of her mother; then using his magic violin, he accompanied Antonia as she sang. Hoffmann returned to find Atonia prostrate on the floor. She died in his arms as he sang her name. Again, lighting threw the shadow of the villain,

Dr. Miracle, across the stage, reinforcing his orchestration of the misadventures Hoffman had suffered.

The stage darkened. When the lights came up for the Epilogue, Augusta had kept it brief. Hoffman knelt alone center stage staring at the empty space where Antonia had been, and Irene as the Muse entered and claimed him as her own. "Earthly love is not meant for you," she sang. "Hoffmann the man is no more. Hoffmann, the poet, arise! I love you, Hoffmann! Be mine!" As he stood slowly and moved toward her, the lights dimmed.

The audience was on its feet even before the curtain drew to a close. Mal put a warm arm around Augusta and said in her ear, "You really did it, Gus. Amazing."

Chapter Twenty-One
A Celebration

Saturday, April 25
11:00 a.m.

"So, is Allan thinking of relocating? Moving into New York?" Milly asked.

"I think he's still pinching himself and enjoying the feeling of accomplishment. He certainly earned it." Augusta smoothed the folds of Milly's wedding dress, preparing to help her don it.

The women looked out onto a beautiful spring day, sunny with a few fluffy clouds drifting across the sky. "What a perfect day," Milly commented. "Did you order it especially for my wedding?"

"I'm very pleased with the delivery," Augusta laughed. "And it's indeed perfect. After the March we had, so far April has been smooth sailing."

Milly, Augusta, and Malcolm had been in the audience at the Metropolitan Opera House only two weeks earlier to hear Allan place second in the Met

Opera audition, a wonderful achievement. And knowing that Luke Bridges was in a maximum security penitentiary eased all their minds.

When they returned home from New York, Milly finally had told Garrett, whose recovery had progressed surprisingly smoothly, they needed to get married—and right now. Augusta asked why she had kept putting off marriage, and Milly replied, "I'm not sure, really. Maybe because my first attempt at being a wife was a total disaster. But I've realized that wasn't entirely my fault, and Garrett and I have really been living together like husband and wife now for several years. Why not make it official?"

Augusta hadn't commented, but it was clear to her the scare of Garrett's brush with death had no doubt helped Milly decide she needed to proclaim to the world her love and commitment to this incredible man whom she had almost lost.

Then had followed a whirlwind of activity for Milly and Augusta, with Martha's help, to put together the intimate wedding ceremony for this day. Garrett, a happy man, made the honeymoon arrangements.

"Did I tell you Allan came to talk to Garrett earlier this week? I mean, a serious talk. Of course he was at the hospital often, and came here once Garrett was released to help however he could. But he wanted to sit down and express his feelings about Garrett most likely saving his life." She paused. "He told Garrett he felt as if he'd gained another father. He said his biological father gave him life, and he would always miss him. But he said when he could have lost his life, Garrett took the bullet. It was the bravest, most selfless thing he'd ever seen."

"That any of us had ever seen. There's a bond between them that will last the rest of their lives."

"There is. Garrett loves Allan as if he were a son. Oh, and get this…Allan went to see Luke Bridges."

Taken aback, August exclaimed, "He went to visit Luke in prison? When?"

"Last weekend. Visitors are only allowed on Saturdays. He wanted to look Luke in the face and ask why he tried to kill him." Milly sat at Augusta's dresser, carefully applying make-up.

"Did he get an answer?"

"He got an earful. All about how Luke had grown up in a family that was different from anything Allan could possibly imagine. A family that extracted revenge on anyone who 'ratted' on them…and Allan and Leslie Jerome had ratted him out by reporting his conduct in Vietnam. He was completely unrepentant about killing Les, and told Allan he shouldn't be sitting there talking to him, but should be dead as well."

"Good Lord. How did Allan respond to that?"

"He told Garrett it confirmed to him he did the right thing by reporting Luke's behavior in the Vietnamese village. He also said Luke is obviously exactly where he belongs, and Allan feels he can move forward with a clear conscience. He knows he was in no way responsible for Leslie's death."

Augusta took a clothes brush from her dresser and brushed Milly's dress.

"Why are you doing that? We just took it out of the bag it was in."

"Fritz. There may have been some dog hair flying around in the air," Augusta replied. "Let's get you into this. We want to start the ceremony in a few minutes, and everyone is gathered downstairs waiting."

Augusta had helped Milly shop for her dress. They had selected a knee-length dress of crepe silk with a matching tunic jacket. The gently flowing skirt was layered, and the wisteria purple color they selected complemented Milly's silvery hair and fair skin.

Augusta, as matron of honor, wore a similar style but in a more subdued, soft blue and a shorter jacket, with matching stilettos, while Milly, ever more practical, wore kitten heels. Once Milly passed Augusta's scrutiny the women headed downstairs to the sounds of happy voices. Milly and Garrett had become family to Augusta's stepchildren, and they were all in attendance, even Maxie, who was ringbearer in a spiffy new Merry Mites suit. Dennis Halloran, considered part of the family, was there as well. Edgar Demarest would perform the brief ceremony, and Allan and Claudia, hand in hand, were also guests.

Since it was an informal wedding, Milly mingled with her friends, Garrett eyeing her appreciatively. He presented his bride with a small bouquet of lavender and white roses and was rewarded with a kiss.

Augusta, Claudia, and Allan went to the piano, and Augusta held up a hand. "Please, everyone, take a seat. Milly asked if Allan and I would sing, and Claudia has been kind enough to play for us. The bride requested one of my favorite songs, 'Du bist die ruh' by Franz Schubert, and Allan arranged it for our duet. Then as soon as the music is concluded, Judge Demarest will perform the marriage ceremony."

Augusta was delighted to have this opportunity to sing with Allan, and the assembled party understood not to applaud but allow the ceremony to begin immediately after the song:

> *You are repose*
> *And gentle peace,*
> *You are longing*
> *And what stills it.*
> *I pledge to you*
> *Through joy and pain*
> *To be a dwelling for you*
> *In my eyes and heart.*
>
> *Come in to me,*
> *And softly close*
> *The gate behind you.*
> *Drive other pain*
> *From this breast.*
> *Let my heart be filled*
> *With your joy.*
> *This temple of my eyes*
> *Is lit by your radiance alone.*
> *O fill it utterly.*

Mal was best man to Garrett, and Augusta stood beside her friend—just as Milly had been her matron of honor some five years earlier, when Augusta married Mal. The ceremony took only a few minutes, and after the judge introduced "Mr. and Mrs. Garrett Stoddard," the happy couple was surrounded and congratulated. Martha disappeared into the alcove to make sure the caterers had the champagne buffet luncheon ready.

Since it was a beautiful spring day, there were tables in the garden, and everyone served themselves and moved outside. Once everyone was seated, Garrett stood and tapped on his champagne glass for their attention.

"First, I want to thank all of you for your well-wishes during my recovery. The visits, flowers, gifts, and cards mean more than you can know." A murmur from the gathering, and Garrett continued. "More than that, though, it means the world to me that you're here with me on what is the happiest day of my life."

He turned to his bride. "Please join me in toasting this remarkable woman, Millicent Devereaux, a lady of vast talent in many ways. A greatly admired pianist, a true *gastronome*, a brilliant teacher, a staunch friend, a woman of wit and wisdom...I'm sure I'm missing something." Chuckles among the party. "I've been asking her to do me the honor of becoming my wife for nearly as long as I've known her. And I am forever grateful as of today to be able to address her as 'Mrs. Stoddard.'"

Glasses were lifted as Mal led the toast, "To Mr. and Mrs. Stoddard."

"Thank you, Garrett," Milly said. "Why is it you always know exactly the right thing to say? Oh wait...I nearly forgot. You're famous for your eloquence, for some reason." Laughter.

Garrett, always one for the last word, remarked, "Well, the only thing left to do now is find a beautiful lady and dash off to Europe with her. Anyone have any ideas?"

More laughter, and Milly joined in. "Since we're not dashing off immediately for Europe, I want to thank all of you for being here to help us celebrate," she said. "Please, let's enjoy this lovely buffet."

Since Milly and Garrett were leaving later that day for their three-week trip to Paris and Vienna, no one lingered. After the bride and groom left, the Mitchell family took care of cleanup. With so many helping it was accomplished quickly and soon the younger members of the Mitchell clan said their goodbyes. After Fritz had been walked and fed, he was temporarily confined to the back of the house.

Mal loosened his tie and removed his jacket, and he and Augusta stretched out on their large, comfortable sofa. Augusta kicked off her blue stilettos and Mal took one foot in his hand, rubbing it.

"Beautiful song you and Allan did. And you sounded great together."

"What a treat to sing with him. It may not happen again; he's going to be a very busy young basso. He's already heard from three opera houses in Germany, and the New York City Opera has offered him a contract for next year for *Don Giovanni* and—get this—*The Tales of Hoffmann*."

"I take it he and Claudia are still together?" Mal picked up her other foot and rubbed it.

"For the present. We'll see what happens with that, especially if he decides to leave Cincinnati. She's happy here even though she might like to do more performing."

"Gus...," he pulled her close, kissing her neck. "I need you to sing for me. That Duparc song, 'Extase.'"

She smiled and caressed his face. "Now why on earth would you want to hear that one?"

"Oh, I don't know...romance in the air today, maybe?"

"You know, Mal, 'Extase' is actually about the aftermath of lovemaking. So really...if I were to sing it properly...."

"Works for me," he said, slipping her dress over her head.

The Case of the Besieged Basso

"SANDY IN THE BOX"

William "Sandy" Sandoz became a Patrolman in 1918 and was immediately transferred to Traffic Bureau, I suspect as a motorcycle patrolman. In 1931, I think, right after the erection of the Terminal, he transferred to District 1 and was assigned as the security for it. He was in a small guard shack for the next thirty years and eventually became known to all as "Sandy in the Box." Factually, he retired in 1961.

Information provided by
Ret. Lt. Det. Stephen Kramer

ACKNOWLEDGMENTS

Now we've reached the year 1970, and life in this country during especially the late 1960s has become turbulent and complicated. I felt I couldn't ignore how the country, and the world, changed during that period.

One big reason for this was the involvement of our military in what was described as a "police action" in the country of Vietnam in Southeast Asia beginning in the early 1960s. We first sent ground troops to the country in 1965. Within a few years our involvement became increasingly controversial, and protests against the war grew and sometimes became violent.

Just before I began writing the Augusta mysteries, I had completed two books about brothers who served in Vietnam—*Memories of Jake* and *Man with No Yesterdays*—and how it affected them and the people they loved. That experience made the Vietnam War my war, in a way.

For any reader who would like to learn more about the Vietnam controversy, I highly recommend Philip Caputo's excellent and painfully honest book *A Rumor of War*. Of all the considerable research I did for those two books, I found this to be the most meaningful.

A character introduced in the second book in the McKee mystery series, *The Case of the Disappearing Director*, was a student at the Conservatory and a fine basso named Allan Meissner who volunteered to serve in Vietnam. When Allan returned after his tour of duty, he struggled to resume his quest for the career he had dreamed of, and was reintroduced in books nine and ten—*The Case of the Casanova Cantor* and *The Case of the Ill-Fated Philanthropist.*

As with many Vietnam veterans, Allan's experiences in that conflict would be a part of him for the rest of his life. Thoughts on how he would deal with one particular incident and its aftermath were the basis of this current book. Interestingly, in real life I was unable to find any opera singer with a major career who had served in Vietnam, though several "pop" singers did.

As always, I have many people to thank for their assistance in the preparation of this novel. First and foremost my remarkable more-than-editor Ashleigh Evans, who as always pointed out sections that needed to move more quickly, or be less "wordy," or needed more, or less, detail. She also manages to control my urges at times to wander off into romance and keeps Augusta—and me—focused on the mystery. I'm so fortunate that she enjoys our collaboration and is personally invested in the series, and in all my books.

Since there is quite a bit of "cop stuff" in this book, I again must thank Cincinnati Police Division retired Lt. Det. Stephen Kramer for his considerable guidance in the many scenes involving law enforcement. It's amazing that he's been my mentor and advisor now for eleven books, and I am forever grateful. While we have shared many thousands of words via email, he at this point remains a long-distance friend…but definitely a friend.

Retired Army Lt. Col. Charles Vincent, who served with the Green Berets in his two tours in Vietnam, assisted with the "incident" that followed Allan Meissner home from his time in Vietnam. Col. Chuck was my consultant and advisor on the two novels mentioned above and I am grateful that I can count him a friend. Who says writing is a lonely profession? Not this author!

Thanks to long-time friend Kristopher Yoder, whom I first knew as a very fine actor, for his assistance with some of the emergency medical information. Kris is now an EMT but continues performing on stage from time to time.

Once again, I am more than grateful to the gifted cover artist Wesley Goulart for providing the beautiful art for this book. Wesley is great to work with and having his art on the cover of now three books is quite special.

When I first ventured into this means of expression after a lifetime in music as student, singer, voice teacher, and director of musical theater productions, a long-ago friend from Oak Ridge (TN) High School provided extensive advice. Michaele Benedict, whom I first knew as a fellow music student in that school and who later became a professional journalist and author, continues to be a source of inspiration for both music and now my attempts at creating books.

Another kind friend, Eric Mark, an actor when I first knew him, has also been a mentor and was among the great people who served as "beta readers" for this book. Thanks to him and also to Audrey Henry, Kathleen Koehler, Marti Lantz, Michael O'Daniel, and Ken Van Camp for their good suggestions which made the book stronger. And perhaps even more, for their assurance that this is a book that readers will enjoy.

Last, my thanks to the Lady Writers of the Poconos, who also read and commented on sections of the book.

Their unending encouragement and our strong friendships are for me a vital part of continuing this journey. Sahar Abdulaziz, Belinda Gordon, Evelyn Infante, Kelly Jensen, and Mary Anne Moore comprise this group and we publish as Shaggy Dog Productions, LLC.

When I wrote *The Case of the Slain Soprano* in 2017, I intended for it to be the first book in a series, but had no thought about how many books might follow. However, it does surprise me that *The Case of the Besieged Basso* is book #11 in "The Augusta McKee Mysteries." This might well be the end of stories about Augusta McKee, but as with each book, I leave that open-ended. Augusta may have more adventures to share with me!

Susan Moore Jordan
Pocono Mountains, Pennsylvania
September, 2024

VIDEOGRAPHY

Selections from *The Tales of Hoffmann*
by Jacques Offenbach
(Note: videos performed in French)

"Olympia's Aria"
Kathleen Kim, soprano

"Barcarolle"
Kate Lindsey, mezzo-soprano, *Nicklausse*;
Ekaterina Gubanova, mezzo-soprano, *Giulietta*
Metropolitan Opera Chorus

"Scintille, diamant" (Shine, Diamond")
Samuel Ramey, basso, *Dapertutto*

Men's trio from "Antonia" Act
Neil Shicoff, tenor, *Hoffmann*
John McCurdy, basso, *Crespel*
James Morris, basso, *Dr. Miracle*

Final Trio from "Antonia" Act
Gabriel Bacquier, basso, *Dr. Miracle*
Joan Sutherland, soprano, *Antonia*
Margarita Lilowa, mezzo-soprano, *Voice of
    Antonia's Mother*

Complete recordings of *The Tales of Hoffmann*
Can be found on YouTube

"Bridge Over Troubled Water"
Paul Simon and Art Garfunkel

(These recordings were available on YouTube as of September, 2024)

The Case of the Disappearing Director

(The Augusta McKee Mysteries, Book Two)

Chapter 1
Witness to Murder

It was a pleasant evening. He stepped off the bus just as the sun was beginning to sink toward the horizon, and paused a moment to enjoy the beauty of the park. It wasn't quite mid-September; the trees were still green with just a few faint hints of color. He turned right past the clear lake, the last of the sunlight glittering on the water, and he could see a sweeping, grassy area, with a gazebo on the far side of the lake.

He turned right again, following a tree-lined walkway that would take him to the Playhouse. Traffic sounds seemed distant. He heard a dog barking somewhere nearby and the faraway sound of a bicycle bell. It surprised him not to see other people out walking, but he knew the Playhouse was near a residential neighborhood. *Dinnertime for those folks, I guess.*

He stepped off the walkway to cut through a stand of trees. *Not much automobile traffic, either.* Just as he emerged from the trees he heard a car speeding in his direction. Almost before he realized what was happening, tires squealed as the car came to an abrupt stop. The car's rear door was flung open and something large appeared to fall out. Or was it thrown to the pavement?

Is it a body?!

Barely comprehending what he was witnessing, he wondered briefly if he should scream for help. Just before the car door slammed shut, he stared directly into the driver's face.

Omigod, omigod, it's—! Shaking, he darted back into the trees, pressing himself against a trunk as he gasped for breath, his mind reeling.

Did he see me? Did he recognize me?

The car sped down the hill, away from the Playhouse.

I have to get away. His heart pounding, his mind in turmoil, he ran as fast as he could back in the direction he had come from. The image of the driver's eyes burned in his brain.

Where can I hide?

The Case of the Purloined Professor

(The Augusta McKee Mysteries, Book Four)

Prologue
Captive

September 11, 1964

Augusta tried again to resurface. Nostrils burning, she managed to get her head above water and gulped in air before going below the surface a second time. Up again, another gulp of air. Her head ached, but now she seemed to be out of the water.

Killer headache. The horizon tipped crazily in all directions. She clutched whatever it was that was under her. A hard surface. Not water. A bed. *I'm lying on a bed.* She began to shiver violently. *So cold.* Her fingers grasped soft fabric. *A blanket.* Clutching the edges, she drew it as tightly around herself as she could.

I'm not in water. I'm not wet. But cold. Freezing.

The shaking subsided. A wave of nausea struck and she swallowed repeatedly, forcing the gorge down. *My eyes aren't working. Why can't I open them?*

Deep breaths. Take some deep breaths. Why does my head hurt so badly?

Breathing deeply helped. The room seemed to lurch, spinning in several directions, but gradually settled. She managed to force her eyes open, squinting, but saw only darkness.

Augusta closed her eyes and continued to breathe deeply, and the nausea eased. She carefully leaned up on one elbow and tried again to peer into the darkness. A small glimmer of light above, close to the ceiling. Shapes and shadows became vaguely visible. Despite the massive headache, she became more aware of her surroundings.

Where the hell am I?

She dragged herself to a sitting position and gingerly swung her stockinged feet over the side of the small bed. A sweet taste in her mouth, not unpleasant. A vague memory of a struggle. She fought to remember more.

Dim light, filtered through a small window near the ceiling, gave no hint of breaking dawn. *It's still night.* Augusta brought her wrist close to her eyes, barely able to make out the hands on her watch. Twelve forty-five.

She had been at a meeting with her production staff at Cliffside College … one of the two colleges where she taught and also directed a spring production. The meeting had broken up late, close to eleven, and she'd stayed behind to organize her notes before leaving the administration building, where her voice studio was located.

The headache, the nausea, the sweet taste. *Dear God, I think I was chloroformed. Like the woman in that case Malcolm told me about. But by whom? And for what reason?*

Peering beyond the bed, she tried to make out what else was in the room.

Two doors, one maybe a closet? And an outside door which I'm sure is locked. I'm being held captive for some reason. By whom, and for what purpose?

Moving on shaky legs, she continued to explore her world. The cement floor was cold through her stockings. *Where are my shoes?* Careful steps to the smaller door. It opened to a small space. In the diffused light she could barely make out the shape of a toilet.

Well, imagine that. An honest-to-goodness water closet. Hopefully, my captor ... or captors ... has also provided toilet paper. All the amenities.

She walked the few steps back to the bed and knelt on it, crawling to the wall where light was filtering in. Standing on the bed, she attempted to look through the window. Something was obscuring her vision, possibly some kind of bush. *No bright lights, and it's quiet.*

Sitting on the bed again, she moved to the edge. *I'm in a residential area, I think. In a room in the cellar of an old house.*

The reality of her situation began to break through the confusion. A cold chill ran through her entire body. *I've been kidnapped. Someone came to Cliffside and waited for me to leave the building, then grabbed me and chloroformed me. I'm being held captive. It's not a bad movie. This is real.* She heard a sound on the other side of the door, a gravelly cough. *Someone is out there. My captor?*

Augusta swallowed hard as she fought back hysteria. *That won't do a bit of good. Think, Augusta. What's that saying—"the best defense is a good offense"?* She recalled times she'd been in danger before and how she had tried to handle it. A grim smile. *Bravado works better when I have my stilettos. Well, I don't have them, I have to manage without what Malcolm calls my "armor."*

She took several deep breaths, steadying herself, preparing herself.

I think I'll let them know I'm awake and royally pissed.

Using her most authoritative tone of voice, Augusta marched to the door and called out: "Whoever you are, I demand you immediately unlock this door and release me."

The Case of the Unearthed Evidence

(The Augusta McKee Mysteries, Book Six)

Prologue

October 22, 1918

It is done.

He leaned against the shovel for a moment, breathing heavily, wiping his sweaty forehead with a shaky hand. *I'll never have to see that face again.*

The wind had picked up and clouds now raced across the moon. He straightened, packed down the earth, smoothing it carefully until he could see no trace of what lay beneath.

Gravel, sand, and stones had been delivered a week earlier. The ground looked exactly as it should, ready to receive the flagstone patio which he would order completed the next day, obliterating forever what he had just done.

No, today. It must be after midnight.

The quiet in his neighborhood was shattered by the repeated sound of a gong—an ambulance racing down Madison Road.

No doubt another influenza victim. He shivered slightly. Cincinnati hospitals had been in crisis mode for nearly two weeks, overwhelmed by those needing immediate care. As an attending physician at General Hospital, he knew that sound far too well.

Four days was all they could spare me. Even for a grieving widower.

Emotions overwhelmed him—grief, rage, despair. He sank to the ground and clutched his head, feeling bile rise in his throat. *What have I done? Killed someone I once regarded as a friend.*

He dragged himself to his feet slowly, leaning heavily on the shovel. He felt he had aged twenty years during the past two hours. The wind grew colder and blew through the trees and shrubs around his house. The sounds of the rustling branches echoed the one word uttered by his victim before he fell to the floor: *Why?*

He glanced around the grounds one final time. No sign of the violence that had transpired. When the masons arrived, completing the work should go smoothly.

As he went inside to clean himself—*though the blood will never come off my hands*—he thought of his adored young son, safe with his aunt and uncle, far away from this city awash in plague and death.

Peter can never know.

The Case of the
Casanova Cantor

(The Augusta McKee Mysteries, Book Ten)

Prologue
A World in Turmoil

Cincinnati, June 1967

The "long, hot summer" of racial unrest in the United States during the summer of 1967 exploded in Cincinnati's Avondale neighborhood on the evening of June 12. Tension had been building in the city since 1965, when the first in a series of brutal rapes and murders remained unsolved. The victims who survived all identified their attacker as Black, though none could identify him.

The situation came to a head with the controversial arrest and conviction of Posteal Laskey, the first viable suspect. Although he was convicted of only one crime, there were many who considered him the perpetrator of the others as well.

The community of Avondale, at one time predominantly a Jewish neighborhood, diversified as people from the Black community moved into the area. Soon enough, unfortunate tensions arose between the two communities. Many in the Black community felt Laskey had been railroaded. Following a tense but peaceful protest meeting that warm June evening, somebody threw a rock, smashing a window. Chaos quickly erupted.

Confirmation rehearsal had just ended at the majestic Rockdale Temple, now past its heyday as a showcase for Reform Judaism in the city. The young people exiting the building soon found themselves caught up in the disturbance.

Eugene Geller, the handsome and popular cantor for the Temple, along with several other adults—and with no little difficulty—managed to get the young people to safety. Once assured his charges were out of harm's way, Gene attempted to return to the Temple to pick up his car.

By then, the street fighting had escalated. Noise, objects, and smoke filled the air as members of the Cincinnati Police Department squared off against the rioters.

Gene did his best to avoid being caught up in the fray. In the confusion of the riot, he kept in the shadows, dashing toward a corner, rounding a building—and disappearing without a trace.

The Cameron Saga

***

Memories of Jake

One brother can't remember. The other can't forget.

Andrew and Jacob Cameron are tied together by a bond more powerful than blood. As young children, they experience a horrific event that tears their family apart. Then just as they complete their high school years, the Vietnam War intensifies. Both young men serve in the military: Andrew in the Marine Corps, Jake as a Green Beret.

Each brother is damaged by his service in Vietnam, Jake in a way that will change his life forever. Andrew, always protective of his rakish younger brother, is determined to restore Jake and their relationship to normalcy. But when Jake disappears, Andrew's life is left in shambles.

His loving parents, his always supportive wife Mary, even his burgeoning career as an artist seem not to be enough to alleviate the pain of Andrew's frantic question:

Where is my brother?

Photo by Dr. Bertram Zarins.
Used by permission.

Man with No Yesterdays

'A thoughtful, superbly paced historical novel
looking at the emotional damage of war.
A FINALIST and highly recommended.'
The 2019 Wishing Shelf Book Awards
A SEMI-FINALIST IN THE
2020 KINDLE BOOK AWARDS
"A harrowing, humane, and inspiring book." - Dave Astor,
Literary Columnist

*"I was born somewhere over the South China Sea in a
military transport plane ..."*

Jake Cameron is facing the struggle of his life. A helicopter crash in Vietnam leaves Jake with total amnesia, and the young Green Beret returns home to a family he doesn't know and a life he can't remember.

Unable to be the son and brother his family has lost, Jake sets out to learn whatever he can about the man he was. When he uncovers a dark family secret, he decides to protect the people he loves by disappearing.

Susan Moore Jordan's new historical novel, MAN WITH NO YESTERDAYS, follows Jake on his journey as he fights to find himself ... a journey that takes him into his past, connects him with other Vietnam veterans, and eventually leads him to situations, places, and a love he would never have dreamed possible.

After a lifetime as a musician—performer, teacher, musical theater director—Susan Moore Jordan wrote and published her first novel in 2013 at the age of seventy-five, and she hasn't stopped since.

In her first four novels, the author drew from her life experiences as a voice teacher and stage director, and those historical novels were inspired by real people she encountered.

"Companion" novels, *Memories of Jake* and *Man with No Yesterdays* were released in 2017. A departure from her earlier historical novels, these two books detail the struggles of two brothers, Andrew and Jake Cameron, whose lives were irrevocably changed by their service in the Vietnam War. *Memories of Jake* was the recipient of an honorable mention Red Ribbon Award from the 2017 Wishing Shelf Book Awards. *Man With No Yesterdays* was a Finalist in the 2019 Wishing Shelf Book Awards.

Jordan next began "The Augusta McKee Mysteries." Book one, *The Case of the Slain Soprano*, was released in April, 2018 and *The Case of the Disappearing Director* followed in October, 2018. Additional books in the series followed, most recently Book #11, *The Case of the Besieged Basso*.

The Case of the Slain Soprano was a finalist in the 2018 Wishing Shelf Book Awards and a semi-finalist for the 2020 Kindle Book Awards. *The Case of the Disappearing Director* was a finalist in the 2019 Wishing Shelf Book Awards.

A third book in "The Cameron Saga," *And This Shall Be for Music*, was released in November of 2022.

The book features the next generation of the family, Andrew's daughter Lindsey, an aspiring opera singer.

All of Jordan's books are "music-centric" (in the words of one reviewer), and readers comment on the strength of the element of music included in her work. Jordan sees writing as another way to share the music she loves, which she considers "the most powerful force in the universe."

Articles by Susan Moore Jordan have appeared in *Musical America* and *The Guardian*, and on August 2, 2019, she appeared on Hour Three of "The Today Show" as a Super Senior.

If you enjoyed
The Case of the Besieged Basso,
please consider leaving a reader review on
whatever site you purchased the book.
Reviews are invaluable to indie authors
and greatly appreciated.
More information and links to all my books
can be found on my website,
www.susanmoorejordan.com